"Let me remind you of something—we don't like each other."

"Correction," Jordan said. "You don't like me. I have no problem with attractive, passionate women. You, on the other hand, have issues—"

"Right." She narrowed her eyes.

"You should feel safe around me," Jordan said easily. "We're practically related."

Right. Jordan's older brother Cole had recently married Sera's cousin Marisa Danieli.

"I'll drive you into the ground, Serenghetti," she harrumphed, changing tactics. "You'll sweat like you've never worked before."

Jordan's smile stayed in place. "I wouldn't expect any less."

"Are you always so sunny?" she grumbled. "Do the clouds ever come out in Serenghetti Land?"

He laughed. "I like to rile you, Perini. I may not have clouds, but I can rock your world with thunder and lightning."

He already had. Once. The fact that he didn't remember just made it all the more galling.

* * *

Power Play is the third book in
The Serenghetti Brothers series.

Dear Reader,

This is my fifteenth book—yay! Over the years, I've enjoyed hearing from so many readers, and the feedback has definitely been reflected in my books. This is also the third book about the Serenghetti brothers—four powerful, passionate Italian American siblings. A double reason to celebrate!

Physical therapist Serafina Perini doesn't reform bad boys, so she's definitely been hexed when she's assigned to injured professional hockey star Jordan Serenghetti. On top of that, she's also now in-laws with the guy thanks to the marriage of her cousin to his brother. And then the situation only gets worse. Because when Jordan comes to her aid after a car accident, she lets herself get caught up in his arms...and he doesn't even remember their steamy past encounter on a beach. Afterward, Jordan can't believe he could have forgotten a woman as hot and passionate as Sera. These days she's a woman he really can't charm. Has he lost his touch—on and off the ice—or is Sera the angel he's been waiting for?

Watch out for more stories about the Serenghettis from Harlequin Desire!

Warmest wishes,

Anna

Website: www.AnnaDePalo.com

Facebook: www.Facebook.com/AnnaDePaloBooks

Twitter: www.Twitter.com/Anna_DePalo

ANNA DePALO

—

POWER PLAY

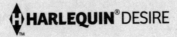

Recycling programs
for this product may
not exist in your area.

ISBN-13: 978-1-335-60390-6

Power Play

Copyright © 2019 by Anna DePalo

Printed in U.S.A.

USA TODAY bestselling author Anna DePalo is a Harvard graduate and former intellectual property attorney who lives with her husband, son and daughter in her native New York. She writes sexy, humorous books that have been published in more than twenty countries. Her novels have won the RT Reviewers' Choice Award, the Golden Leaf and the Book Buyers Best Award. You can sign up for her newsletter at www.annadepalo.com.

Books by Anna DePalo

Harlequin Desire

CEO's Marriage Seduction
The Billionaire in Penthouse B
His Black Sheep Bride
One Night with Prince Charming
Improperly Wed

The Serenghetti Brothers

Second Chance with the CEO
Hollywood Baby Affair
Power Play

Visit her Author Profile page at Harlequin.com, or annadepalo.com, for more titles.

You can find Anna DePalo on Facebook, along with other Harlequin Desire authors, at Facebook.com/harlequindesireauthors!

For my editor, Charles Griemsman.
Your editorial guidance has been invaluable!

One

Sera disliked smooth operators, bad in-laws and unwelcome surprises.

Unfortunately, Jordan was all three, and his sudden appearance in her offices on a sunny spring day in Massachusetts meant she'd better start preparing herself for the unthinkable.

"You!"

The exclamation was out of Sera's mouth before she could stop it. It had been just another day at Astra Therapeutics until Mr. Hotshot-NHL, Underwear-Ad-Hottie Jordan Serenghetti had crashed the party like an errant puck arcing through the air.

Jordan smiled lazily. "Yes, me."

Arms folded, he lounged against the treatment table, as if striking sexy poses was second nature to him—

even when propped up by crutches, as he was now. Clad in a casual long-sleeved olive T-shirt and jeans, he emanated charisma. The shirt outlined the hard muscles of his arms, and the jeans hugged lean hips. Not that she was noticing. Not in *that* way.

Sera was wary of men who were too good to be true—as if everything came easy to them. Nowadays, Jordan Serenghetti would be at the top of her list. He was smoother than a skate blade hydroplaning over ice. With dark, ruffled hair clipped short, moss-green eyes, and a sculpted face with a chiseled jaw, he could score anywhere.

Sera had seen him in underwear ads, showing off his package on supersized billboards and fueling thousands of dreams. But she'd learned the hard way to deal in reality, not fantasy.

"What are you doing here?" she blurted, even though she had a sinking feeling she knew. She'd been told her next appointment was waiting for her in room 6, but she'd had no idea it was Jordan.

She'd heard he'd suffered a sports-related injury, but figured he was in good hands with the New England Razors hockey-team staff. She *so* was not going to worry about him, even if her *second-worst mistake* was now related to her by the marriage of her cousin to Jordan's brother. In the annals of her bad history with men, Jordan ranked number two, even if it had become clear to her that he didn't remember their chance encounter in the past.

She eyed his wrapped left knee. She wasn't used to seeing Jordan Serenghetti vulnerable…

"Now, that's a refreshing change from the usual

greeting. Too often I get enthusiastic fans yelling my name." He shrugged. "You're an antidote to the monotony, Angel."

Sera sighed. Fans? Women screaming his name was more like it. *Terribly misguided, deluded women.* "Don't call me Angel."

"Hey, I'm not the one who named you for a heavenly being."

She'd never had occasion to rue her name so much. *Serafina* served as a topic of easy cocktail-party conversation, but the nickname Angel irked her, especially when uttered by Jordan. So what if she was named for the seraphim?

"Your type of angel is supposed to be heavenly and fiery," Jordan went on, unperturbed. "Someone had a kismet moment when they named you. Beautiful and hot-tempered."

Serafina rolled her eyes, refusing to be swayed by the way *beautiful* rolled off Jordan's tongue. "Am I supposed to be impressed by your grasp of biblical trivia… or backhanded compliments?" Then she scowled at the thought that her response had just proven his point. She dropped her clipboard on the counter. "So you're here for a physical-therapy session…"

"Yup."

She quelled her irritation. "And I'm supposed to think it's mere chance that you were assigned to me?"

Jordan held up his hands, a smile teasing his lips. "No, I'm not going to lie about that part."

"Oh, good."

"I want the best—"

Sera was sure Jordan was used to the best in women.

No doubt eager females were waiting for him when he exited the New England Razors' locker room.

"—and you've already got a great reputation. The clinic manager couldn't stop singing your praises."

With a pro athlete of Jordan's caliber, Sera was sure Bernice had given him his choice of staff. And the clinic's manager probably thought she was doing Sera a favor...

Sera thought back to her conversation earlier in the week with Bernice. *We're trying to land a contract with the New England Razors. Their management is looking to outsource some therapy work and supplement the team's staff. They're auditioning three outfits, including us. If we land this deal, it could open the door to work with other sports teams in the area.*

Ugh. At the time, she'd dismissed her chances of encountering Jordan, even though he played for the Razors. The gods couldn't be so cruel. Apparently, however, gods laughed at angels. Jordan had been sent—or volunteered—to test the quality of the clinic's services. With her. She should have known the minute she stepped into this room, but she'd been in deep denial.

"You asked for me?" Sera said slowly.

Jordan nodded and then cracked a grin. "The fact that, when I booked my appointment for today, your receptionist couldn't stop extolling your cooking skills just sealed the deal for me."

"She mentioned my cooking?"

"And baking," he added. "Apparently, the home-made dishes that you sometimes bring in for the staff earn you brownie points. So you were clearly the right choice."

"Let me remind you of something…we don't like each other."

"Correction," Jordan said, lips quirking. "You don't like me. I have no problem with attractive and passionate women. You, on the other hand, have issues—"

"Right." She narrowed her eyes.

"You should feel safe around me," Jordan said easily. "We're practically related."

Right. Jordan's older brother Cole had recently married Sera's cousin Marisa Danieli. Jordan loved to joke about the couple's long and winding path to the altar. At one point, Marisa's former fiancé had been dating Cole's ex-girlfriend, and Jordan had kidded that his brother and Marisa were engaged by proxy. It did *not*, however, mean that *she* and Jordan were related in any meaningful sense of the word.

Up to now, Sera had done her best to ignore the fact that she and Jordan were technically cousins-in-law. Marisa and Cole had had a surprise wedding, so she'd been spared having to be the maid of honor to Jordan's best man.

"I'll drive you into the ground, Serenghetti," she harrumphed, changing tactics. "You'll sweat like you've never worked before."

It was only a half-idle threat. She expected a lot from her patients. She was good, she was understanding, but she was tough.

Jordan's smile stayed in place. "I wouldn't expect any less."

"Are you always so sunny?" she grumbled. "Do the clouds ever come out in Serenghetti Land?"

He laughed. "I like to rile you, Perini. I may not have clouds, but I can rock your world with thunder and lightning."

There it was again. The sexually tinged double meaning. And then a traitorous voice whispered, *You already have. Once.* The fact that he didn't remember just made it all the more galling. "You don't want to get involved with me." *Again.* "I'm not a woman you can conveniently walk away from." *This time.* "I'm your sister-in-law's cousin."

He arched a brow. "Is that all that's stopping you?"

She threw up her hands—because no way was she going to remind Jordan about the past. *Their past.* And with her bad luck, in the future she and Jordan would be named as godparents to the next Danieli-Serenghetti offspring. As it was, they'd dodged that bullet the first time around since Jordan's brother Rick and his wife Chiara had done the honors. It seemed Cole was going down the line by order of birth in naming godparents from among his siblings.

Jordan shrugged and then glanced around. "At least we'll have the memory of a few good physical-therapy sessions."

"All you'll be remembering fondly is the pain," she practically snarled.

"I'm a good listener if you ever want to...you know, talk instead of spar."

She swept him a suspicious look—unsure if he was joking or not. *Better not to take chances.* "As if I'd open up to a player like you," she scoffed. "Forget it."

"Not even when you're off duty?" he teased. "It could be therapeutic."

"When I need to unwind, I'll book a vacation to the Caribbean."

"Let me know when you're going. I'll reserve a seat."

Argh. "It's a vacation—as in, I don't want to be irritated!"

He quirked an eyebrow. "Irritated isn't your natural state?"

"No!"

"So where do we go from here?" he said. "You're irritated…"

As he said the words, Jordan watched Serafina with bemusement and not a little lust. With blond hair swinging past her shoulders and amber eyes, she was a knockout. He'd been around plenty of beautiful women, but Sera's personality shone like an inner light. Of course, she directed snark at him, but he enjoyed tangling with her.

She was a puzzle he was interested in solving. Because if he'd ever met a woman with a boulder-sized chip on her shoulder, it was Sera Perini.

"Listen, I'll make you a deal," he joked. "I'll try to behave if you stick around and help me out."

"You will behave," she said firmly. "And your coupon is valid for today's session only. After that, the sale is over."

His eyes crinkled. "Hard bargainer."

"You have no idea."

"But I guess I'm going to find out."

"True, but first you need to sit on the treatment table so we can take a look at that knee." She paused. "Let me help you."

"No need."

Even though they were now related by marriage and had seen each other at the occasional family gathering, they'd never come close to touching. Not a pat, not a brush of the arm, and certainly not a peck on the cheek. *Nada.* It was as if by tacit agreement boundaries had been drawn, because they were more like warring in-laws than the friendly kind. And maybe because they understood that, it was dangerous to cross some unspoken line.

Now, bracing his arms, he hopped up onto the table using his good leg.

"Nice stunt," she commented drily.

He tossed her a jaunty grin. "More where that came from."

With a last warning look, she turned her attention to the paperwork he'd brought with him to the appointment and had dropped on the counter before she'd walked in.

He took the opportunity to study her again. Today, she wore nondescript, body-concealing light blue scrubs. When she'd sometimes waitressed at the Puck & Shoot, the popular local sports bar, she'd usually kept her hair pulled back in a ponytail or with a headband and had had a black apron tied around her waist. But thanks to the fact that they were now related by marriage, he'd seen her in other getups: body-skimming dresses, tight-fitting exercise attire... She had an hourglass figure that was fuller on top, so everything flattered her. More than once he'd caught himself fantasizing about what it would be like to run his hands over her curves and skim his palms over her endless legs.

Yet he didn't know what to make of her. He was attracted as hell, but she was an in-law…and she didn't like him. Still, the urge to tease her was as natural and unavoidable as breathing, and as irresistible as the impulse to win a hockey championship. And on top of it, he needed her physical-therapy skills. Already the companies behind his endorsement deals were getting nervous because he'd been off the ice. For the umpteenth time, he pushed aside the thought that his career could be over. He'd work like hell in therapy to make sure that possibility would never become a reality. Sure he'd made some savvy business investments with his earnings, but his plans depended on continuing to play.

With a grimace, Jordan turned and stretched out his legs in front of him on the treatment table.

Sera looked up, seemingly satisfied with what she'd gleaned from his intake papers. "So how did the ACL tear occur?"

"A game three weeks ago against the New York Islanders. I heard a pop." He shrugged. "I knew what it was. Cole's been through this before."

His older brother had suffered a couple of knee injuries that had ended his professional hockey career. These days, Cole was the head of Serenghetti Construction, having taken over after their father's stroke had forced Serg Serenghetti to adopt a less active lifestyle.

"You're lucky it happened at the end of the hockey

season, and the Razors didn't advance in the playoffs this year."

"I've never thought of getting knocked out in the playoffs as a lucky break," he quipped. "Especially when I wasn't there to help."

"It's a tear, not a break," she parried. "So who performed the ACL surgery on your knee?"

"Dr. Nabov at Welsdale Medical Center, and it was last week. In-patient for a day. They insisted I stay overnight. I guess they didn't want to take any chances with my recovery. Hockey fans, you know."

"Mmm-hmm." Sera flipped through his paperwork again. "Did you sign autographs while you were there?"

He cracked a smile and folded his arms over his chest. "A few."

"I assume the nursing staff went wild."

He knew sarcasm when he heard it and couldn't resist teasing back. "Nah, they've seen it all."

"You've been icing the knee?"

"Yeah. The staff at the hospital told me what to do postsurgery."

"Until you could get yourself into more expert hands?"

He flashed a grin. "You. Right."

She might totally be his type if she wasn't so thorny... and since she was related to him by marriage, a casual fling was out of the question. Still, there were layers there, and he enjoyed trying to peel them back.

Sera set aside his paperwork and approached him, her expression all business. "Okay, I'm going to unwrap your knee."

For all her prickliness up to now, her touch was light

as she removed his bandages. When the bandage was off, they both studied his knee.

"Good news."

"Great."

"No signs of infection and very little bleeding." She pressed on his knee as he remained in a sitting position on the table but leaned back propped up by his arms.

"Am I hurting you?" she asked, not looking up.

"Nothing I can't handle."

"Manly."

"We hockey players are built tough."

"We'll see." She continued to press and manipulate his knee.

"I'm your first. Otherwise you'd know."

"I've never been curious about how tough hockey players are."

"You're mentally disciplined."

"We physical therapists are built tough."

Jordan smiled. "Built pretty, too."

"Behave."

"Right."

Then she reached over to the counter for an instrument. "I'm going to take some baseline measurements so we know where you are."

"Great." He waited as she straightened his knee a little, measured, and then bent his leg and measured again.

After putting the measuring instrument aside, she said, "Okay, not a bad starting point considering your knee has been wrapped since surgery. Our goal today is to improve your quad function and the mobility of the patella, among other things."

"What's a *patella*?"

She tucked a strand of hair behind her ear. "Your kneecap."

"Of course."

"Let me know if I'm causing you too much pain."

Her tone was surprisingly solicitous, so he joked, "Isn't that what you promised? Pain?"

"Only the intended and expected variety."

He was a high-level athlete—he was used to pain and then some. "How many ACL tears have you treated?"

"A few. I'll let you know at the end if you were my best patient."

He stifled a laugh because she'd deftly appealed to his competitive instincts. He wondered if she used the same technique to cajole all her patients. Probably some played sports—since a torn ACL wasn't too unusual an athletic injury—even if she'd never treated a professional hockey player like himself before. "Will you dock me points for irreverence?"

"Do you really want to find out?" Methodically, she taped two wires to his thigh. "I'm going to set you up with some muscle stim right now. This will get you started."

In his opinion, they'd gotten started with the electricity when she'd walked in the room. But he sensed that he'd teased her enough, and she wasn't going to take any more nonsense, so he kept mum for the next few minutes and just followed her directions.

After the muscle stim, she taught him how to do patellar glides. He followed her instructions about how to move his knee to gain more flexibility. They followed that up with quad sets and heel slides, which she told him to do at home, too.

Overall, he found none of it too arduous. But at the end of half an hour, she announced that his ability to bend his knee had gone from around ten degrees to eighty.

He grinned. "I'm your best?"

"Don't flatter yourself, Superman. Your knee was wrapped in bandages that interfered with motion until now, so you were bound to make some significant improvement."

"I'll take that as a yes."

"You're impossible."

"No, I'm very possible if you'll consider your options. Now, insufferable, that's another thing…"

Sera seemed to grit her teeth. "You'll need weekly appointments."

"How long will my therapy last?"

"Depends on how it goes." Her expression was challenging—as if she'd been referring to his behavior, good or bad, as well as his recuperation. "Usually three to four months."

"Nothing long-term, then?"

She nodded. "What you're used to."

A fling. The words drifted unspoken between them. She'd met his double entendre and raised him. *Ouch.*

Two

"I can't do it. There's no way I can be Jordan Serenghetti's physical therapist." Sera drew her line in the sand. Or rather, on the hockey ice—or *whatever*.

"You have to," Bernice, the clinic's manager said, her short curly brown hair shining under the overhead fluorescent light.

"He needs a babysitter—" *of the centerfold variety* "—not a trainer. Or a physical therapist."

"We're counting on you to help us land this client."

And Jordan Serenghetti was counting on landing her. His appointment had ended over an hour ago, and still she was suffering the lingering effects. Annoyance. Exasperation. Indignation. She'd spent the time since naming her emotions.

True, Jordan emanated charm from every pore. She

wasn't immune. She was still a woman who liked men, and she wasn't dead. And okay, maybe she was the one with long-suppressed needs. But that didn't mean Jordan was getting anywhere with her. *Again.* She still remembered the feel of his lips on her. And he didn't have any recollection—*none whatsoever.* She'd just been another easily forgotten face in a cast of thousands. That much had become clear once she'd re-encountered him years later while waitressing at the Puck & Shoot, and there'd been not even a flicker of recognition in his eyes.

She knew the score these days, and this time she was determined that the game would end Sera 1, Playboy 0.

Endure months of close contact with Jordan? It would test her nerves and more. So after her session with him had ended, Sera had sought out Bernice in her office to plead her case. Standing just inside the doorway, she focused on the bobblehead dolls lining her boss's bookshelves. All the major sports were represented there—including hockey. Scanning them, Sera didn't see Jordan. It gave her hope that she had a small chance of convincing Bernice. How big a fan could her boss be?

"How about you reassign me and I bring you another baked lasagna to thank you?" Sera cajoled.

"Ordinarily I'd consider a small bribe," Bernice parried, her desk chair turned toward the office's entrance, "especially if it's one of your homemade dishes. But this time, no. The staff has been enjoying the big pan of baked ziti you brought in for lunch today, though."

Sera lowered her shoulders.

"If we do a good job," Bernice continued, "we

should get regular business from the New England Razors. It'll be a huge boost for Astra Therapeutics and for your career."

Sera held back a grimace. As far as her boss was concerned, there'd be no getting out of this gig.

Bernice tilted her head. "You've dealt with difficult clients before. We all have."

Sera opened and closed her mouth. This was different. *But she could hardly explain why.* "Isn't this like nepotism? I get the plum client because he's related to me by marriage?"

Bernice chuckled. "The fact that you're practically family should make this assignment a piece of cake." Her manager looked thoughtful. "Or if he's a bad in-law, well then, we've all had those, too."

Sera pressed her lips together. *Damn it.* She'd worked so hard to get her physical-therapy degree. She'd moonlighted as a waitress and endured three grueling years back at school for a graduate degree. And now Jordan Serenghetti stood in the path of her advancement.

Bernice gave her an inquisitive look. "On the other hand, is your problem that Jordan has too much magnetism? Some people get starstruck by celebrities and have a hard time focusing on the job."

Sera spluttered. "Please. The fake charm is a big turnoff."

Her manager raised her eyebrows.

Sera's face heated, and she quickly added, "I'm not taking it personally. There isn't a woman alive Jordan doesn't try to charm."

"You know, if I were a little younger, and my husband would let me, I'd consider dating Jordan Seren-ghetti."

"Bernice, please! You've got gold with Keith. Why trade it in for pyrite?" Sera knew her manager had just celebrated her sixtieth birthday and thirtieth wedding anniversary.

"What makes you think Jordan isn't genuine?" Bernice countered.

Sera threw up her hands. She wasn't about to dig into her past with her boss—and explain how she'd honed her instincts about men the hard way. She was wise enough these days not to be taken in by ripped biceps—hadn't she seen them up close an hour ago?—and hard abs. Probably those lips were still magic, too. "The problem is he knows he has the goods."

Bernice laughed. "There's nothing wrong with a man who's confident."

"Try arrogant." Sera knew she had to talk to Marisa. Perhaps her cousin could convince Jordan that this work arrangement wasn't a good idea. If she couldn't get out of this assignment herself, maybe Jordan would back out.

Knowing she wasn't going to get anywhere with Bernice, Sera decided to back off and change the subject. But when her workday ended at four, she made the short drive from Astra Therapeutics' offices outside Springfield to Marisa and Cole's new home in Welsdale.

Sera pulled up to a classic center-hall colonial and thanked her lucky stars for May in western Massachusetts. The breezy, sunny day could almost erase her mood. She had texted Marisa in advance, so when she got out of her beat-up sedan, her cousin was already opening the front door.

Marisa wore a baby sling and raised a finger to her lips but exchanged a quick peck on the cheek with Sera. "Dahlia just fell asleep. I'm going to lay her down in her crib and be right with you."

"You and Cole have gone all Hollywood with the baby naming," Sera remarked wryly, because even months later, the baby's name brought a smile to her lips.

"If Daisy is acceptable, why not Dahlia?" Marisa said over her shoulder as Sera closed the door and followed her into the house.

"And here I thought Rick and Chiara would go all name crazy, but no, nope, they had to settle on something traditional like Vincent." Frankly, it wouldn't have surprised her in the least if the middle Serenghetti brother and his new wife, actress Chiara Feran, who resided in Los Angeles most of the time—home to the weird Hollywood baby-naming craze—had come up with something like Moonlight or Starburst.

Sera bore only a passing resemblance to her cousin. They shared the amber eyes that were a family trait, but she'd grown a shade taller than Marisa by the time she was fourteen—and her dark blond hair set her apart from her cousin, who had long curly brown locks. When Sera had been younger, she and Marisa had been deep in each other's pockets, and sometimes she'd wished the similarities had been strong enough that they could easily pass as sisters.

"I'll be right back," Marisa said as she started up the stairs from the entry hall. "I'll meet you in the kitchen."

As Sera made her way to the back of the house, she noted once again that it bore the stamp of domesticity. The new home was still sparsely furnished, but the signs of baby were all around. She figured that Jordan must break out in hives here.

When her cousin came back downstairs moments later, Sera put down her glass of flavored water and braced her hands on the granite kitchen countertop. She wasted no words. "Marisa, Jordan is about to become a client of mine."

Her cousin's expression remained mild as she turned on a baby monitor. "They're sending him to you to help recover from his torn ACL."

Sera didn't mask her surprise. "You know? And you didn't warn me?"

"I found out just this morning. Cole happened to mention Jordan was heading to Astra Therapeutics. But I wasn't sure he would definitely be assigned to you." Her cousin wrinkled her brow. "Though, come to think of it, he did make an offhand comment to Cole about possibly asking for you…" She shrugged. "We thought he was teasing because, ah, you two have always seemed to rub each other the wrong way at family gatherings."

"Well, it's no joke, but someone has made a mistake." Wanting to spare her cousin any awkwardness with her in-laws, and because, frankly, her first encounter with Jordan had been embarrassing, she'd never mentioned to Marisa that she and Jordan had briefly crossed paths in the past. It was bad enough that others could sense tension between her and the youngest Serenghetti brother.

"If anyone can whip Jordan into shape, it's you," Marisa teased.

Sera scowled as she pushed away from the kitchen counter. "This isn't funny."

"Of course not, but maybe you've met your match."

Sera shuddered. "Don't say it."

The last thing she needed was for anyone to think Jordan was a work challenge that she couldn't conquer. First off, she didn't want to conquer anything—especially him. Second, no way was he her *match* in any other sense of the word—not that Marisa could mean *that*. The fact that Jordan had found her infinitely forgettable at twenty-one was evidence enough that they weren't fated *in any way*.

Her cousin glanced down at some paint chips fanned out on the kitchen counter. "Who knew there were so many shades of beige for a guest bedroom?" she asked absently. "I just want a soothing tone, and Cole is kidding me about using Diaper Brown."

"Is that the name of a paint color?"

Marisa pinked. "Paint colors are a running joke in this house ever since Cole and I redid the kitchen cabinets in my old apartment."

Her cousin and her husband had only months ago moved into the new colonial in Welsdale that Cole had built for their growing family. They'd moved in right before Dahlia was born, and Sera knew that the process of decorating weighed on Marisa, especially as a new mom. "Most of us can use a professional. Get a decorator."

Marisa looked at her thoughtfully. "Isn't that why Jordan is coming to you? Because you're a professional?" She tugged on the hem of her top and rubbed at a stain. "Why are you so reluctant to help him?"

Sera opened her mouth and then clamped it shut. Because…because… No way was she getting into any embarrassing past *incidents*. "He's obnoxious."

"I know you two have a testy relationship, but he'll have to do what you tell him."

"He's a smooth operator." *Happy-go-lucky.* With a bad memory to boot. And he didn't know the meaning of struggle.

Marisa glanced at her keenly. "You're protesting too much."

"Paraphrasing Shakespeare? Spoken like a true English teacher."

"Former English teacher. And I'm on maternity leave from the assistant principal position at the Pershing School." Marisa yawned. "Something to eat?"

"No, thanks. And you're doing great in your leave as a new mom."

Her cousin gave a rueful laugh. "I know, but family history and all. At least Cole is on board."

Sera gave her cousin a reassuring pat. Marisa had been raised by a single mom, Sera's Aunt Donna. Marisa's father had died before she'd been born—having already made clear that a baby didn't factor into his plans for pursuing a minor-league baseball career and maybe getting to the majors.

Men. These days, Sera didn't need more confirmation that they could be fickle and untrustworthy. Her awful experience with Neil had taught her enough. Jordan had just been the start of her bad track record—one she seemed to share with the women in her family.

Must be in the genes. "You and Cole have to convince Jordan this is a bad idea."

"Sera—"

"Please."

Jordan shifted in his seat next to his brother and glanced around the crowded bar. Business was humming as usual on a Thursday evening at the Puck & Shoot. None of his teammates from the Razors were around, partly because many had scattered for home or vacation in the postseason.

Sera also no longer moonlighted here as a waitress— and *that* was a good thing, he told himself. He could still recall his reaction when he'd first discovered, shortly before Cole's marriage, that the hot blond waitress at his favorite dive was Marisa's cousin. The fates had a twisted sense of humor.

Still, tonight, even without his teammates and Sera at the Puck & Shoot, it almost felt like old times. He nearly felt like his old self—*normal*. Not injured and off the ice, with brothers who'd suddenly morphed into fathers—though he was happy for them. It felt good not to be holed up at home, which would have just given him more time to mull his uncertain future and push away his regular companion these days—unease.

If he could only take out his frustration and pent-up energy the way he normally did, things would be better. "Man, I miss our evenings at Jimmy's Boxing Gym."

Cole, sitting on the bar stool next to him, smiled. "I've got better things to do with my after-work hours these days."

"Ever since you got hitched, you've become boring,

old man," Jordan grumbled good-naturedly. "And fatherhood has just added to your—" he strangled out the word "—domesticity."

"Dahlia is brilliant," Cole countered. "Did I tell you she rolled over the other day?"

"No, but she clearly takes after Marisa. Beauty and brains."

Cole just smiled rather than giving as good as he got—and that was the problem. Jordan wished for the old days. It was as if his brother didn't even miss hockey. What was the world coming to?

"The only reason I'm here at the Puck & Shoot is because of Marisa," Cole said. "She's the one who encouraged me to come keep your sorry butt company."

"You owe me one. More than one. You might not be wallowing in wedded bliss if it weren't for me."

"Yeah, how can I forget." Cole's voice dripped sarcasm. "Lucky for you, it all ended well. Otherwise, you could have been sporting a broken nose."

Jordan grinned because this was a spark of the old Cole he was used to. "Luck had nothing to do with it. You and Marisa were destined to be together. And for the record, a broken nose would have just added to my sex appeal."

Jordan had seen how unhappy his older brother had been when his reconciliation with Marisa had headed south, so he'd fibbed and told Cole that Marisa was looking for him—sending his unsuspecting brother to her apartment. Jordan had hoped that once the two were alone, they'd have a chance to talk and patch things up. They'd realize they were made for each other. In fact, Cole and Marisa hadn't made up then, but shortly afterward. And in the aftermath, they'd invited everyone to an engagement party that had turned out to be a surprise wedding.

Sera had been at the event, of course, looking sexy and tempting. He'd only discovered at a fund-raiser a short time before that she was Marisa's relative; there he'd recognized the attractive waitress from the Puck & Shoot whom he'd never had a chance to speak with and who always seemed to avoid him. The physical resemblance when she was side by side with her cousin had been unmistakable.

He'd gone slack-jawed, however, at Sera's transformation from waitress to temptress in a blue satin halter-top cocktail dress. Makeup had enhanced her unique and arresting features—full lips, bold eyes and fine cheekbones that any model would have wept for. And the halter top on her dress had emphasized her shoulders and toned arms before skimming down over testosterone-fueling curves to endless legs encased in strappy, high-heeled sandals. Seeing an opportunity to make his move, he'd approached the two women, but Sera had swatted him away like a pesky fly that night...

Cole slapped him on the back. "You look pensive. Buck up. It's not all doom and gloom."

Jordan didn't think his thoughts were showing, but maybe he was wrong. "Since you got married and gave up the mantle to become nauseatingly cheery, someone has to take over the role. And now both you and Rick are fathers."

Cole's face broke into a grin. "Yup."

"Someone has to uphold the family reputation."

"What reputation are you referring to? Being depressed and down?"

"No. Sexy and single." If he wasn't a professional hockey player and all-around chick magnet, who was he? He gave an inward shudder. Best not contemplate the abyss.

"All right, but from the looks of you, I've got to ask. What's throwing shade on sexy and single?"

Jordan waved his beer. "The obvious."

His latest injury had kept him off the ice for the end of the season, and his corporate partners—with contracts for endorsement deals—were starting to get restless. Not to mention his injury didn't put him in a great position to negotiate his next contract with the Razors. Everyone knew that one Serenghetti had already had a career-ending ACL injury.

"I'm proof there is life after the game," Cole said quietly.

"Yeah, I know, but if I can get over this injury, I should have a few more good seasons left." He was on the wrong side of thirty, but he was still at the top of his game. Or rather, he had been. In the last couple of years, he'd shifted position from right wing to center and had had some of his best seasons ever. The one that had recently ended might have been just as good, except it had ended abruptly for him with a knee injury. Still, at thirty-one, he figured he could squeeze out another half decade at the top—if he had better luck than in the past weeks.

"Speaking of injury," Cole said, nodding to the crutches that Jordan had propped against the bar, "what's your game plan for this one?"

Jordan took a swig of his beer. Fortunately, since it was his left knee that had needed surgery, he'd been able to start driving again this week. "I'm doing physical therapy."

Cole took a swallow of his own beer without glancing at him. "Yup, I've heard. Sera. So you weren't joking when you mentioned it might be her you'd see at Astra…"

"News travels fast," Jordan murmured. "I was just in to see her yesterday."

"And I'm supposed to be here to convince you not to see her."

Jordan tossed his brother a quick look. "Wow, so this is what it feels like."

"What?"

"The first time a woman has tried *not* to meet me."

"Sera is special."

"Tell me about it."

"You don't want to tangle with her. She's Marisa's cousin and not someone you can easily walk away from."

"Hey—" Jordan held up his hands "—all I'm asking is that she cure my knee, not date me." So what if Sera had already made a variation of Cole's argument?

His brother's tone was light, but there was also an undercurrent of warning. He wasn't sure whether the note of caution was because Cole was thinking about Jordan's best interests, or because he was naturally protective of his wife's relative. Cole had always been the responsible one, *relatively speaking*, and Jordan had chalked it up to oldest-child syndrome.

"Face it, Jordan. You can't turn off the charm. You love to get a rise out of Sera."

"I thought I was helping her career by asking for her."

"Apparently she doesn't want the boost."

Jordan twisted his lips in wry amusement. If he didn't have a healthy ego, he'd be feeling a twinge of wounded pride right now. "Look, when the Razors' management discovered I'd need physical therapy, they wanted me to try out a new outfit for them. I remembered Sera worked at Astra Therapeutics, so I mentioned the only name I knew when it was time to set up an appointment."

"Except Sera doesn't want to work with you."

Jordan put a hand to his chest. "Be still my heart," he said mockingly. "A woman who doesn't want me."

"You'll get over it. Trust me, you don't want to get involved with Marisa's cousin. I've seen her in the boxing ring. She throws a mean left jab."

"Which one?" Jordan joked. "Marisa or Sera?"

"Sera, but take my word for it, it's in the genes."

"And you know this how?"

Cole gave a long-suffering sigh. "Marisa and I met Sera at her gym once before having lunch nearby. She was finishing up her workout." His brother's lips quirked. "The rest I know because I'm married to one of the parties involved. Marisa is no pushover herself."

So Sera boxed. Like him. Interesting. She liked to take out her frustrations on a punching bag?

Still, Jordan quieted. He hadn't expected Sera to go to the trouble of recruiting Marisa and Cole to make her case. He'd thought he was doing her a good turn by asking for her by name. He was surprised by her level of opposition, and not for the first time he wondered what was behind it. Maybe he should let her off the hook about this physical-therapy gig if she was that panicked about it. But possibly not before finding out why she was so dead-set against him...

Three

"Guess what?"

Sera regarded her older brother, Dante, with a wary eye. There'd been many *guess what*s in their lives. *Guess what? I brought your hamster in for show-and-tell... Guess what? I'm dating your volleyball teammate... Guess what? You're getting your own car—my old wreck.* She loved her brother, but sometimes it was hard to like him.

This time, they were at Dory's Café in downtown Welsdale, and she had some major armor against an unwelcome surprise. Namely, she was sitting down, already fortified by morning coffee ahead of brunch. And Dante was lucky—there was a table between them, so she couldn't kick him in the shins as she might have done when she was six—not that she was above trying if things got out of hand.

"Okay," she mustered, "I give up. What is it? Winning lottery numbers? One-way ticket to Mars? What?" She stuck out her chin and waited.

"Nothing so dramatic, sport." Dante chuckled. "New job."

Sera breathed a sigh of relief. "Congrats. That makes two of us in less than three years. Mom will be doing the happy dance." Frankly, her mother could use good news. Rosana Perini was still putting the pieces of her life back together—rearranging the puzzle that had broken and scattered when she'd become a young widow. The whole family had needed to regroup when Joseph Perini had died six years ago when Sera was twenty-three. It was one of the things that had made Sera decide to start a new chapter in her life by going back to school for her physical-therapy degree.

"You're looking at the new VP of Marketing for the New England Razors."

Sera's stomach plummeted as she was jerked back to the present. No, no and *no*. Dante's working for the New England Razors meant only one thing: another connection to Jordan Serenghetti. Still, she managed to cough up the critical word. "Congratulations."

"Thanks, Sera. It's my dream job."

Her brother had always been a sports nut. His teenage bedroom had been decorated with soccer, football and hockey memorabilia. No wonder someone had thought he was perfect for the Razors marketing position.

A dream come true for Dante. A nightmare for her.

She didn't need her life further entangled with Jordan Serenghetti's. Her brother would be offering up free game tickets and suggesting a family evening out. Or talking nonstop about Jordan Serenghetti's prowess—on and off the ice.

Dante, though, appeared oblivious to her discomfort. "I wonder if Marisa can grease the wheels for me with Jordan Serenghetti. You know, maybe invite us both to a family barbecue at her house again soon." Her brother shrugged. "Making sure that Jordan and the Razors are happy with each other is part of my new job description."

"She doesn't need to," Sera managed to get out, volunteering the information because Dante would find out eventually anyway. "I'm seeing Jordan myself."

Dante's eyebrows shot up. "Oh, yeah?"

"Jordan is my new client at Astra Therapeutics. The Razors are farming out some of their physical rehab, and Jordan is their guinea pig."

A grin split her brother's face. "You mean your guinea pig."

Sera tossed her hair. "Hey, I'm a professional."

"Then why do you eye him at family gatherings as if he's the first case of the plague in five hundred years?"

"Professional distance."

Dante snorted. "I'll buy that as fast as a counterfeit trading card on an online auction site."

"Whatever. I'm giving him the boot to another therapist in the office."

"Why?"

"You just said it yourself. We don't get along."

"What about family loyalty?"

"To Jordan Serenghetti? He's only a cousin-in-law." As if she could forget.

"Jordan could end up owing you a debt of gratitude for getting him back on his feet."

Just then, the waitress arrived with their food—a lumberjack breakfast of eggs, sausage and toast for Dante, and an egg-white omelet for her. Sera liked to practice what she preached to her clients—healthy eating and clean living. She also made sure to thank the waitress because she knew what it meant to be on your feet for hours.

Her brother took his first bite and then tilted his head and studied her. "You don't like him because women fawn over him."

"I hadn't noticed, and anyway it's none of my business." She gave all her concentration to seasoning her food with the pepper mill.

"You shouldn't let one bad experience with what's-his-name Neil sour you."

True…if she could trust her instincts. But she still wasn't sure her radar was working right. And Dante had no clue that she and Jordan had shared more than casual conversation in the past. Not that she wanted her brother to ever find out. It was bad enough he knew the basics of her drama with Neil.

Dante waved his fork as he swallowed his food. "You should at least tell Jordan that your attitude isn't personal."

"Never…and you're not going to, either." Because it was personal—and wasn't just about her unsavory experience with Neil.

"Okay, play it your way, but I think you're making a mistake."

She shrugged. "Mine to make."

"Ser," Dante said, suddenly looking earnest, "I could use your help."

"Wow, this is a change."

"I'm serious. I need Jordan back on the ice, and the sooner the better. It would make a great start to my new job if I could claim some credit. Or at least if I could say my sister—the physical therapist with the golden touch—helped get him back in shape."

Sera made a face. "Ugh, Dante. That's asking a lot."

Dante cleared his throat. "I got the position with the Razors…but there's already a higher-up who is gunning for me." He shrugged. "We have some bad history together at a prior employer, and I'm sure he'd be happy if I screwed up."

Sera sighed. "What kind of bad history?"

Her brother looked sheepish. "We were in competition at a sports agency…and there might have been a woman involved, too."

Great. She took a bite of her omelet. She could just imagine her brother involved in a love triangle. *Almost.* She didn't want any more details.

"Fans come to see Jordan in action," Dante cajoled.

"Whatever." From what she could tell, Jordan was still in fantastic shape despite his injury, and she didn't care how much money he had on the table. The guy had major bank already—what was a few million, more or less, to him?

"Sera, I'm asking."

Sera shifted in her seat. Because, for once, the tables were turned. Her brother needed her help—unlike when he'd stepped in to bail her out when they were younger. Sure, he'd been a thorn in her side with his antics—keeping her on edge—but he'd also cast a protective mantle. Unlike her, Dante remembered the child their parents had lost at birth, and it was almost like he'd absorbed their unspoken worries about losing another loved one. So, he'd issued warnings about situations to avoid at school, stood up for her when she'd been picked on as a kid and, yes, kept some of her secrets from their parents.

On the other hand, Jordan threatened the safe and tidy world that she'd worked hard to build for herself. She knew just how potent his kisses could be, and she was nobody's fool. Not anymore. If she stepped up for Dante, she'd be walking a fine line...

Sera folded her arms as she stepped into the examining room. "So you're stuck with me."

Jordan was leaning against the treatment table, crutches propped up next to him. He was billboard-ready good-looking even under the fluorescent lights of the room. She, on the other hand, was in her usual shapeless scrubs. Clearly, if he didn't enjoy toying with her, she'd be beneath his notice—which ran to models, actresses and reality stars these days, if his press was to be believed.

Jordan's expression turned to one of surprise, and then he gave his trademark insouciant grin. "I'm stuck with you? And here I thought the best part of the day was getting to sample your cannoli bruschetta mash-up recipe along with the rest of the staff. It was delicious, by the way."

"Well, you were wrong," she deadpanned. Why did she feel a thrill at his compliment?

"What prompted the change of heart? Don't keep me waiting. This is the most suspense I've had in ages."

"I'm sure it's a rare occurrence for a woman to keep you cooling your heels."

Jordan's smile widened. "What do you think?"

She ignored the question and gritted her teeth instead. *Best to get this over with.* "My brother, Dante, just got a job with the Razors. Marketing VP, to be exact."

Jordan raised his eyebrows and then his lips quirked. "You Perinis can't seem to stay away from professional hockey players."

She gave him a frosty smile. "Let me remind you that I was initially recruited for this job. I didn't volunteer."

"The end result is the same."

"Now I'm helping out Dante by getting you back on your feet."

"Of course."

Well, that was easy.

"Do I get anything in return for helping you out?"

Sera narrowed her eyes. She'd spoken too soon. This was more like the Jordan Serenghetti she expected. "Don't be evil. The chance to spread some beneficence should be good enough for you."

Jordan laughed, looking not the least bit insulted. "Now I understand why you showed up for my appointment today as scheduled—instead of, you know, feigning typhoid or something."

"Count your blessings."

"So you're going to agree to be my physical therapist, and here I was about to let you off the hook."

"You're not going to make this easy for me, are you?"

"Is that a rhetorical question?"

"The silver lining is that I get to make you sweat."

"Some people pay to see that, you know."

Of course she knew Jordan got paid millions for his skills on the ice. Still… "Don't you ever stop?"

"Not when it's this much fun."

"Well then, I guess it's time for me to stop making it so enjoyable for you."

"You know, I really was going to let you off the hook today." Jordan shrugged. "Cole came to see me because you were adamant about not being my therapist. Obviously, you've had a change of heart."

Now she looked like an opportunist. She didn't know that Marisa had followed through and told Cole to have a talk with Jordan. "Why didn't you cancel your appointment? Or ask for someone else before your scheduled time?"

"I didn't want you to look bad at the office. I figured it would be better if the word came from you."

Sera lowered her shoulders. She felt bad—guilty… Damn him. She was only trying to help her brother!

Jordan just stood there, being himself—all sexy. Badass abs and chiseled pecs under a formfitting T-shirt, square jaw, magnetic green eyes and all.

Sera gritted her teeth again. She could do this. She… owed him. "Thanks."

He cupped his hand to his ear. "What was that?"

And just like that, they were back to squabbling. She knew she was rising to the bait, but she couldn't help herself. "Thank you…for giving me the opportunity to see you grunt and sweat."

Jordan laughed but then started leveraging himself onto the treatment table. "Ready when you are."

She moved aside his crutches and then helped him stretch his legs before him. When he was settled, she examined his knee. After a few moments of poking and prodding, she had to admit he was coming along nicely. "The swelling is about as good as we can expect at this stage."

"So I heal well?"

She looked up. "You're a professional athlete at the top of your game. It's not surprising." When he looked pleased, she added, "Today we're going to focus on increasing mobility and improving your quad function even more."

"Sounds…fun," he remarked drily. "You know, it's amazing we didn't know each other in high school. You lost some opportunities to kick my butt."

"*Amazing* isn't the word I'd use." *More like a relief.* Her teenage self could have gotten into big trouble with Jordan. As it was…but she was older and wiser now.

"Marisa mentioned you grew up in East Gannon. Right next door."

"And yet a world away." East Gannon was Welsdale's poor cousin. People had small clapboard homes, not mansions with expensive landscaping.

Jordan looked thoughtful. "Welsdale High played East Gannon plenty of times."

"I didn't pay much attention to hockey in high school. I left that stuff to Dante."

Jordan's expression registered surprise. "And you call yourself a New Englander?"

She stuck out her chin. "I played volleyball."

Jordan's eyes gleamed. "An athlete. I knew there must be something we had in common."

Sera stopped herself from rolling her eyes.

"And you also box to stay in shape, from what I understand," he murmured. "So two things we have in common."

"I doubt there are three," she countered, and he just laughed.

She could get used to the way his eyes crinkled and amusement took over his entire face.

"You went to Welsdale High?" she added quickly. "I figured you'd gone to a fancy place like Pershing School along with Cole."

Cole Serenghetti had been a star hockey player at the Pershing School. It was where he'd met Marisa, who'd attended on scholarship. They'd had a teenage romance until Marisa had played a part in Cole's suspension. Then they'd led separate lives for fifteen years until fate and a Pershing School fund-raiser had brought them together again.

"Serenghetti Construction wasn't doing well during a recession, so I decided to take the financial burden off my parents by switching to Welsdale High for my junior year."

"Oh." She tried to reconcile the information with

what she knew of Jordan Serenghetti. *Self-sacrificing* wasn't a word that she'd have associated with him. And she didn't want a reason to like him.

Jordan gave her a cocky grin. "I had an excellent run at Welsdale High School. You missed it all."

"No regrets." Then, giving in to curiosity, she asked, "Do you ever wish you'd gone to Pershing School?"

"Nope. Welsdale High had just as good a hockey team, and we were the champs twice while I was there."

This time, Sera did roll her eyes. "No doubt you think it was due to the fact you were on the team."

Jordan smiled. "Actually, I was a lowly freshman for the first win."

She shrugged. "Maybe you thought Pershing School was second-best to Welsdale. After all, the suspension that Marisa earned Cole meant that Pershing hadn't won a championship in a while."

Jordan held up his hands in mock surrender. "Hey, I don't blame Marisa. She had her arm twisted by the fates." He gave her a cheeky look. "And no, I didn't transfer because I thought Welsdale High had a better hockey team. I figured whichever side I played on would have the superior team."

"So I was right, after all. You claim all the credit."

Jordan relaxed his teasing expression. "As I said, since the two teams were about equal, I decided to do my parents a favor by saving on tuition. But I let them believe that the hockey team was the reason for my switching schools."

Sera got serious, too. "Well, it was a nice thing to do. Apparently, you do have a pleasant side…occasionally."

He angled his head. "Want to help me brush up on my manners?"

"I'm not a teacher, and something tells me you'd be a poor student. But actually, right now I have something to show you."

He perked up.

"Heel slides," she said succinctly, all business. "The first exercise for your knee."

"Oh."

She guided him in a demonstration of sliding the heel of his foot along the treatment table, extending his knee for twenty seconds. After that, as he reclined on the table, he did repetitions by himself while grasping a belt that was anchored with the heel of his foot.

"Great," she said encouragingly. "This should improve your quad function."

He grunted as he continued, until she felt he'd done enough.

She took the belt from him and put it aside on the counter. "Now I'm going to teach you something you can do at home by yourself."

He arched a brow, and she gave him a stern look even as she felt heat rise to her face.

"Great," he managed. "I suppose I should be glad that there are no paparazzi around, angling for a picture of me on crutches."

"Exactly." Putting her index finger at the location of one his incisions, she moved her finger back and forth, her touch smooth but firm. "This scar massage is to reduce inflammation. You should continue to do this daily." She started a circular motion. "You can also vary the direction."

Sera kept her gaze focused on his knee, and Jordan was quiet for a change—watching her.

"So I have a question," he finally said, his tone conversational. "Have any of your clients flirted with you? Before me?"

"We haven't flirted. Well, you have, but it takes two to tango." With an impersonal touch, she placed his hand where hers had been on his knee. "Now you try."

He inclined his head in acknowledgment, imitating her motion. "Okay, what about before me?"

She covered his hand to guide him a bit, ignoring the sudden awareness that came from touching him again. "Some have tried, none have succeeded."

"Wow, a challenge."

"You would see it that way. But nope, a futile endeavor is more like it."

He looked up. "Throwing down the gauntlet."

She met his gaze. "You're too incapacitated to bend low enough to pick it up."

"But not for long," he replied with a wicked glint.

"Now we're going to try the stationary bike," she announced, ignoring him.

Jordan raised his eyebrows. "I'm going to be biking already?"

"Your good leg will be doing all the work." She was relieved they were moving to the wide-open gym. Verbally tangling with Jordan Serenghetti while they were alone was like walking a tightrope—it took all her focus, and she needed a break.

He followed her over to the gym on his crutches, and she helped as he gingerly got on the bike.

Because he exuded so much charisma, Sera could

almost forget Jordan was injured. She refocused her attention and instructed him in what to do.

He slowly pedaled backward and forward with his right leg, his left knee bending and straightening in response.

"How's the pain?" she asked.

He bared his teeth. "I've had worse in training sessions with the Razors."

"Good. You want to push but not too hard."

"Right."

She watched him for a few more minutes until she was satisfied with his effort. "Good job."

"Effusive praise from you," he teased.

"We're not done yet," she parried.

After several more minutes, they returned to the treatment room, where she instructed him on how to do straight-leg raises while resting on his back. She followed this up with having him do raises from the hip while he was lying on his side. Then she helped him sit up to do short arc quads, raising his leg from the knee.

As he was finishing up his last exercise, she glanced at the clock and realized with some surprise that their time was up.

She tucked a stray strand of hair behind her ear and exhaled. "Okay, that's it for today."

He raised his brows. "I'm done?"

She nodded. "You're making excellent progress. You've gained some more motion in your knee since the surgery, and that's what we're going to continue to work on."

He smiled. Not mocking, not teasing, just genuine, and Sera blinked.

"Glad things are working out," he said.

That made two of them. For her peace of mind, Jordan couldn't get well fast enough.

Four

"The companies behind the endorsement deals need reassurance. When do you think you'll be playing again?" Marvin Flor's worried voice boomed from Jordan's cell phone.

Jordan shifted on his sofa. Marv had been his agent since his professional hockey career had started nearly ten years ago. He was good, tough and a whiz at promotion. Hence Jordan's promotional contracts for everything from men's underwear to athletic gear and sports drinks. Marv was in his sixties and a dead ringer for actor Javier Bardem—and well into his third decade as a top-notch sports agent.

"Why don't you partner with your sister, Mia, for a line of men's apparel? Isn't she an up-and-coming designer?"

Jordan stifled a laugh, pushing aside the thought that Marv's half-joking suggestion—at least, he thought it was only semiserious—might be a sign of desperation. His house phone rang, and he ignored it. "First off, I don't think Mia's ready to branch into men's sportswear just yet. And second, we'd throttle each other if we worked together. Sibling rivalry and all that."

Jordan gazed at the lazy, late-afternoon sunlight filtering through the floor-to-ceiling windows of his Welsdale penthouse. Usually in the off-season, he was a whirlwind of energy. Vacationing in Turks and Caicos, making personal appearances…working out to keep fit. Now the weights in his private gym lay unused, and he hadn't met Cole at Jimmy's Boxing Gym in weeks. At least he'd been able to shed his crutches the other day, since he was close to four weeks postsurgery.

Marv sighed. "So, okay, what's the latest on when you'll be back on the ice?"

"Doubtful for the beginning of the season. We're looking at three months of therapy at least." Jordan winced. His endorsement contracts had clauses in them, and if he wasn't on the ice, he'd stand to lose a cool few million. And then there was the upcoming negotiation of his contract to continue to play for the Razors…

"What's the prognosis?"

"There's no reason not to expect full recovery." *At this point.*

Jordan could almost hear Marv's sigh of relief.

"Good. Because everyone is aware of the family history."

Meaning Cole. Meaning ACL tears ran in the fam-

ily. And had been career-ending for at least one Serenghetti already. Not good. "I'm in great hands, Marv.
The best." He couldn't complain about his doctors. His
physical therapist, on the other hand...

Sera had surprised him at their last session. He was
happy to help smooth Dante's way with the Razors.
And Sera was going to be his reluctant physical therapist for the duration...even if she sometimes acted as
if she wanted to take a few shots at him in the boxing
ring. The thought made Jordan smile. In fact, the biggest problem with his prolonged recovery was that his
plan for what to do with the endorsement-deal money
might be in jeopardy. He'd had a few restless nights
about his career hitting the rocks, but he was a fighter.

"Well, if we can't get you on the ice, we need to
keep you in the public eye with a positive spin," Marv
continued. "That should help keep the companies that
you've partnered with happy."

Jordan heard his landline ring again and told Marv
to hold on even as he picked up the receiver with his
free hand. After building reception announced that his
mother was on her way up, Jordan switched back to his
agent. His day was about to get more interesting, and
Jordan knew he had to wrap things up with some quick
reassurances. "Don't worry, Marv. With this banged-
up knee, I'm not likely to be partying hard in Vegas."

"Yeah, yeah. But good press with your name attached to it would be better. It's not enough to stay
out of trouble."

Jordan knew Marv would love his plan for what to
do with the paychecks from his endorsement deals,
but he wanted to keep his idea to himself for the mo-

ment. He hadn't mentioned his intentions to anyone, and anyway, good publicity and Marv's worries weren't the reason he wanted to go ahead with his plan. No, his reasons were deeper and personal, which was why he'd kept a lid on his goal till now.

"I suppose a semiserious relationship isn't in the cards."

Jordan coughed. "No."

He intended to enjoy his pinnacle of fame and fortune. He'd spent enough years being the sickly kid who'd been stuck at home—or in the hospital. That was, until he'd grown into a solid teenager who could slap the puck into the goal better than anyone.

On top of that, his current lifestyle wasn't conducive to home and hearth. He was on the road half the time when he was playing, and the NHL season was long in comparison to other sports. He wasn't ready to settle down. He was still Jordan Serenghetti—NHL hotshot and billboard model—despite his temporary detour. He'd spent years on the ice. He wasn't sure who he was beyond the identity that he'd taken a long time to carve out for himself.

Marv grumbled. "Well, at the moment you are staying in one place for a while. There's hope. A relationship with a hometown sweetheart would give us some positive ink in the press. Work with me here."

The only woman Jordan was seeing lately was Sera…and she was hardly the type who'd be mistaken for his girlfriend, given that her typical expression around him was a scowl. She'd probably slam the door in a paparazzo's face—and then issue a vehement denial and threaten litigation about linking her good name to Jordan Serenghetti. The last thought made him smile again.

He figured they could have some fun together—what was the harm in a little flirtation? And he was curious about the basis of Sera's prickliness. At least it should make her happy that he'd been doing the exercises that she'd assigned for him. He was also looking forward to seeing her next week—sparring with her and peeling back some more of the layers that made up the complex and intriguing Serafina Perini.

Jordan heard the private elevator that led straight into the penthouse moments before the door opened and his mother appeared, casserole dish in hand.

"Gotta go, Marv," he said before ending the call on his agent's admonition to keep in touch.

Jordan straightened, lowering his bad leg from where it was resting on the sofa's seat cushions. "Mom, this is a surprise."

Everyone but his mother knew better than to show up unexpectedly.

Camilla Serenghetti smiled as she stopped before him. "I brought you something to eat."

Because his mother still bore traces of an Italian accent—as well as having a habit of mixing words from two languages in a single sentence—the *eat* came off sounding as if there was a short *a* vowel at the end of it.

"Mom, it's my knee that needs help, not my stomach." Still, whatever she'd brought smelled delicious.

"You need to keep up your strength." She moved toward the kitchen where a Viking range was visible from the living area. "Lasagna."

"With béchamel sauce?"

"Just like you like it."

"The staff on the show must adore you if you're always sharing special dishes." *Like someone else he knew.* Except his mother had her own local show, *Flavors of Italy with Camilla Serenghetti*—her name had been added to the title in recent years.

His mother turned back from the kitchen and frowned. "It's not because of the staff that I worry. It's the new television station owners. I'm not sure they like my cooking."

"You're kidding."

"There's talk, *chiacchierata*, about big changes. Maybe no cooking shows."

"They're considering canceling you?"

Camilla's hands flew to her cheeks. "*Per piacere*, Jordan. *Please*, watch what you say."

Jordan knew this show was his mother's baby. And his father had made a guest appearance—finally coming out of the funk into which he'd sunk after his stroke.

"Mom, they're not going to cancel you. They'd be crazy to."

"Not even if they want to bring the television station in a new *direzione*?"

"You mean *take* the station in a new direction." He was so used to correcting his mother's English, it was second nature. She'd been doing a mash-up on her adopted language as long as he could remember.

"*Take, bring*, whatever. *Open* the light means *turn on*. You understand me, *si*?"

Jordan smiled. "More importantly, your viewers

understand and love you. You speak the international language of food."

A look of relief passed over his mother's face. "Years of trying recipes on my family paid off. And you ate my *pastina con brodo*. Always. Good kids make great cooking skills."

He loved his mother's pasta in broth. He'd grown up on it. Even today, the aroma of it brought him back to childhood. He'd been served the dish every time he'd been ill or injured—anything from the common cold to the more serious episodes that had landed him in Welsdale Children's Hospital.

He also knew how much the show meant to his mother as far as giving her a late-life second act. Jordan schooled his expression. "How's Dad? Besides drowning in *pastina con brodo*, I mean."

His mother served the same dish to every ill family member. And because his father had never fully recovered from his stroke, his mother could continue with her culinary cure-all indefinitely. In fact, Jordan was surprised she hadn't brought more of her signature dish with her today on her visit to his apartment.

"Giordano, don't be fresh. Your father is okay with his health. The show, not so good."

Jordan relaxed a little at news of his father. Serg Serenghetti's health had been a cause for concern for his family ever since his stroke a few years ago. For his mother's benefit, however, Jordan teased, "Next you'll be telling me that you're vlogging to build up your audience."

"No, *mia assistente* on the show already does it for me."

"And a star is born." He was surprised his mother even knew what vlogging was, but he supposed he shouldn't be astonished that a cooking show would have already been posting videos online.

"Hmm. Tell that to your father."

Jordan crinkled his eyes. "What does that mean? You just said Dad was fine."

"Yes, with his health."

"Wait, don't tell me... He's having a hard time with the fact that you're the breadwinner now?"

"You know we don't need the money."

"So what is it?" Jordan kept the smile on his face.

For once his mother looked hesitant. "I think—"

"Your star is outshining his?"

Camilla nodded. "He suggested a regular segment about wine on my show. Starring him."

Jordan bit back a laugh. "Delusions of grandeur."

"He built Serenghetti Construction," his mother pointed out.

"Right." Frankly, the wine-segment scheme seemed right in line with his father's outsize personality. "Rope him in, Mom, before he can get away and strike a deal with bigger fish. Cole can get you a lawyer. Tie him up with an exclusive arrangement." He was joking—sort of.

Camilla looked heavenward as if asking for divine intervention. "We already have a long deal. We're married."

Jordan shifted on the sofa, masking a grin.

When his mother's gaze came back to him, she swept him with a sudden, appraising look. "You seem better. More robust. Sera is doing therapy for you."

It was a statement, not a question. His mother was more in the know than he'd realized.

"Yes, what a coincidence," he said cautiously as he straightened, slowly and deliberately.

"Such a lovely woman."

Here we go. But he refused to rise to the bait. "Yup, Cole inherited a great set of in-laws."

"She could have provided rehabilitation for your father."

"Too late. Besides, Dad's stroke happened before Marisa reconnected with Cole." Grimacing, he started to rise, and as he expected, his mother transitioned from hovering in front of him to moving forward, filled with concern.

"Careful, don't hurt yourself. You still need to finish healing."

He waited while she placed a helping hand under his elbow before he stood fully. "Thanks, Mom."

Rick might be the Hollywood stuntman and his new sister-in-law Chiara an actress, but it didn't mean he couldn't call upon his own acting powers when necessary—like diverting his mother from a topic full of pitfalls.

Stepping back, his mother said, "Come and eat."

Mission accomplished.

Why was she here tonight? Her days moonlighting at the Puck & Shoot were supposed to have ended long ago when she'd become a physical therapist. But she was still being roped into helping out from time to time when the bar was short-staffed. She just couldn't say no to the extra cash.

Balancing a tray of beers, she kept sight of Jordan out of the corner of her eye.

Angus, the bar's owner, had called in desperation because they were down two waitresses, and it was going to be a busy Saturday night. The Puck & Shoot was the type of place where the saltshaker was either nearly empty or ready to shower your fries in an unexpected deluge. Still, the regulars loved it.

The part-time gig had helped pay for her education, but at some point, the tables had flipped so that the job was what was holding her back from starting her new life—one which she'd thought involved *not* seeing certain regulars. But she felt she owed Angus.

Jordan sat at the bar, as usual, and held court with a couple of Razors teammates who happened to be around even though hockey season had ended. Sera recognized Marc Bellitti and Vince Tedeschi.

Since Jordan had a habit of not taking a table, she'd almost never had to serve him. It had been years since their brief encounter during spring break in college, and when she'd first started working at the Puck & Shoot, it had become clear that Jordan hadn't recognized or remembered her. She'd been angry and annoyed and then somewhat relieved—especially after Neil had confirmed her opinion about certain types of men. They were players who moved from one woman on to the next, juggling them like so many balls in the air.

Now that Jordan knew who she was, though—Marisa's cousin and his new therapist—even the little bit of distance afforded by his customary seat at the bar seemed woefully small. As she served the beers to a table of patrons, she was aware of Jordan filling the room with his presence. He had that high-wattage magnetism that celebrities possessed. With his dark green gaze, square jaw and six-foot-plus muscled frame, he could make a woman feel as if she were the only one in the room. *Damn it.*

And Sera knew she wasn't imagining things. More than once, she caught his gaze following her back and forth across the crowded bar. It made her aware of her snug-fitting T-shirt and short skirt only partially hidden by an apron. Even though she wasn't dressed up or showing much skin, she wasn't in the shapeless light blue scrubs she wore at Astra Therapeutics, either. And her hair caught back in a ponytail for convenience just meant that she couldn't hide her expression from Jordan.

Already she was regretting her decision to stay on as Jordan's therapist—news that she'd broken to Marisa in a brief text. Only sheer strength of nerves had gotten her through a total of four therapy sessions with Jordan so far—and counting. In the past two weeks, he'd shed his crutches—though he still wasn't close to being completely recovered, of course. In therapy, he'd done the exercises that she'd shown him, including doing hamstring stretches, using a stationary bike and walking on a treadmill. They'd worked on gaining balance, extension and strength in his knee—with a minimum of quips thrown in.

She admired his powers of recuperation. She ought to be pleased. And yet…her only defense was that she was in charge during their sessions. He was all taut, lean muscle—in his prime and in great shape.

After making sure that everyone at her table was satisfied with their order, she wound her way back across the bar with her now-empty tray. She again tried to shake off the prickly sensation of being watched in a sensual fashion. Jordan had done it in the past, before he'd known who she was, but now it was more pronounced—blatant, even. It should have been the opposite since they were in-laws. He *knew* she couldn't be just a casual hookup, because they'd see each other again. Didn't the guy ever obey a DANGER sign?

She frowned. She ought to remind him about what had happened during spring break eight years ago. She'd been tempted to on several occasions, but her pride had stopped her. The last thing she wanted to do was tell Jordan that she'd been one in a long line of forgettable women.

From the periphery of her vision, she noticed a young brunette sidle up to Jordan and strike up a conversation. After a moment, Jordan smiled and slid into flirtatious mode. *Naturally.*

Sera belatedly recognized the other woman as Danica Carr, an occasional patron. Not too long ago, she'd been approached by Danica with questions about getting into a physical-therapy program. Angus had told Danica that Sera had worked her way through school by waitressing.

Sera determinedly ignored Jordan and his new friend and kept busy as the bar got more crowded. The distraction of work was a relief, but almost an hour later, she had the beginnings of a low-grade headache. It was a lot of effort pretending Jordan didn't exist. And he was *still* talking to Danica.

As she paused at the corner of the bar at the end of her shift, Sera felt her temper spike, or at least lick the edges of her conscious. She untied her apron and stuffed it behind the counter. Once upon a time, she'd been Danica. Young, trusting and on the cusp of making a significant career choice.

These days, she didn't even go on dating apps. All that swiping left at the end of a long day was exhausting. If she couldn't trust her instincts about a guy even after months of dating, how could she put her faith in a mere photo on her phone?

Jordan was probably a dating-app star. The thought popped into her head, and she could feel her mouth stretch into a sour line. Whether Danica knew it or not, Jordan was a lion playing with a kitty, and Sera suddenly knew it was up to her to be the lion tamer. She couldn't stand by and do nothing while another naive young woman got taken in by Jordan Serenghetti.

Sera watched as Danica walked away and rejoined her party at their table. Straightening away from the bar, Sera moved toward Jordan, and at the last moment, he turned his head and noticed her—almost as if he'd known all along exactly where she was.

He was dressed in jeans and a crewneck T-shirt that showed off his biceps—how did he manage to be a walking billboard even injured? His gaze flicked over her, quick but boldly assessing, missing nothing from her breasts to her hips. Still, she refused to be unnerved or to succumb, where most mortal women would be tongue-tied and giggly.

When she stopped in front of him, Jordan remained silent, watchful, his expression for once indecipherable. Fortunately, Marc Bellitti and Vince Tedeschi were caught up in their own conversations at the bar and seemed too distracted to notice.

"Danica is a naive kid," she said without preamble. "Move on. She's not in your league."

Jordan smiled. "You know my league?"

Serafina pressed her lips together. Jordan Serenghetti really was beyond redemption—not that she was in the savior business. "I don't do bad boys. My mother taught me right."

Jordan's expression bloomed into a grin that shot straight through her. "Straitlaced. You need to loosen up."

Ha! Easy for him to say. He was the guy who was nothing but loose...and went over like smooth cocoa butter with most women.

Though not with me, she reminded herself. *Not anymore.* "And for the record, you're my patient. It's all business between us."

He glanced around him. "We're in a bar, not at Astra."

"But I'm still working."

He rubbed his chin and then teased, "You're not a woman who's bowled over by my charm?"

"Of course not. Far too levelheaded." *These days.* It was hard to explain how she'd fallen prey to Neil not so long ago, but maybe she'd been overdue for a lightning strike... Then again, the more she thought about it, the more she wondered whether she'd fallen for Neil precisely because he'd been smooth and worldly and sophisticated. Maybe she'd been determined to prove that she could play in the big leagues and wasn't help-less little Sera who needed protecting.

"And yet, I sense fire and passion in you," Jordan murmured.

"That's because I put you in the hot seat, Seren-ghetti. I see right through your game."

He made a show of glancing around him. "You've stolen the Razors' playbook?"

Sera placed her hands on her hips. It wouldn't be good if Angus noticed her in an argument with a customer—particularly a famous hometown favorite—but fortunately the bar was packed. "You know what I mean. I know your type, and I can read your plays off the ice."

"Jealous of Danica?"

"Please."

He swept her a look that she felt everywhere. "You shouldn't be, you know. At the moment, prickly wait-resses seem to be my type." He regarded her thought-fully. "Particularly those that might have had a prior bad experience."

Sera sucked in a breath and clamped her lips to-gether. He didn't know the half of it. "I'm not naive, if that's what you're suggesting."

"I didn't claim you were. But you are...wary."

Yup. Once bitten, twice shy.

Jordan searched her expression and then relaxed his. "Danica isn't my type, but I make it a policy to be nice to fans."

As if on cue, Danica suddenly reappeared. "Jordan, I'm leaving—" she looked eager as a puppy "—and I was wondering, do you need a lift home?"

Jordan gave a killer smile that made Sera want to reach for a pair of sunglasses. "I'm good."

"Oh." Disappointment was etched on Danica's face. "I thought with you being injured and all..."

"I'm off crutches and can drive." Jordan waved his hand at Sera, and the other woman noticed her for the first time. "It's what Sera and I were discussing."

Sera tossed him a speaking look. *Oh, really?*

Danica pushed her dark straight hair off her shoulder. "Hi, Serafina."

"How are those physical-therapy program applications coming along?" Sera asked, dropping her hands from her hips.

Danica's face fell. "I still need a prerequisite or two. I'm never going to pass Chemistry 102."

"Sure, you will. With lots of studying. Then you can spend your days bending players—" she gestured at Jordan "—into shape."

Jordan looked amused. "I need to be straightened out apparently."

"More like set straight," Sera muttered, her gaze clashing with his.

"Oh." Danica looked between them. "Sorry, I didn't know."

Sera blinked. "Know what?"

A small frown appeared on the other woman's brow. "Um..."

Jordan got off the stool, and in the next moment, Sera felt his arm slide around her shoulders.

Danica took a step back and then another. "Well, I think I'll be going." Turning back in the direction where her friends were still waiting, she added quickly, "Nice talking to you."

Sera twisted toward Jordan. *What had just happened?* "You let her think—"

"Yeah, but you gave me the opening."

Sera pressed her lips together.

"Thanks for allowing me to let her down easy."

"I didn't—"

Jordan slanted his head. "You warned her off me. Goal accomplished."

"Not like that!" She didn't want Danica to think that she and Jordan were… *Oh, no…no, no, no. Never. No.*

Jordan leaned in, his face all innocent. "Like what?"

She spluttered. "You know what."

He lowered his gaze to her mouth. "It's what you said."

She bit back a gasp. "You're blaming me?"

He gave a slow, sexy grin. "Thanking you. Let me know when you're ready to…explore what's between us."

Sera had never been in a more frustrating conversation in her life. "Nothing more ego-stroking than the idea of two women competing for your attention, huh?"

"If you say so."

Suddenly, she'd had enough. Enough of a guy who could juggle women with dexterity—even injured.

"You don't remember," she snapped.

"Remember what?"

"Spring break in Florida eight years ago."

Jordan's lips curved. "Am I supposed to?"

"It depends," Sera said sarcastically. "Do you keep a running tally of the women you dally with, or do they just run together in one seamless and nameless high-light video in your mind?"

Jordan tilted his head, looking more intent. *"Dally with?"*

She gestured with her hands. "Flirt with. Come on to… Kiss."

"I'm supposed to remember every woman I ever flirted with?"

"Granted, it must be a long list. How about kissed?"

"Including the fans who've thrown their arms around me?"

She drew her brows together. "Including the ones you've chatted up on spring break and engaged in some lip-to-lip action with after a couple of beers."

Jordan regarded her thoughtfully. "Are you saying we've kissed…and I don't remember it?"

Sera smacked her forehead. "Give the man a prize for a light-bulb moment."

Jordan grinned. "It must have been some kiss."

"You don't remember it!"

"But you do."

Sera felt herself heat. "Only because you've become famous."

He frowned. "I would have remembered an unusual name like yours."

"I didn't give you my name, and anyway, you probably would have thought I meant *S-A-R-A-H*." It was a common mistake that she was used to.

"So you like to operate anonymously?" he said, enjoying himself.

"I'd just turned twenty-one." *I was young and stupid.*

Jordan rubbed his chin. "Let's see, eight years ago… college break. Destin, Florida?"

"Right," she responded tightly. "Hundreds of students clogging the beach. Beer flowing. Dancing. You angled in…"

They'd locked gazes while she'd danced, and the sexual attraction had sizzled. In swim trunks and with all his smooth, tanned muscles, he'd been an Adonis. And she'd never felt sexier than when he'd looked her over in her aqua bikini, appreciation stamped on his face, and had started dancing with her.

She'd known he wanted to kiss her and had met him halfway when he'd bent, searching her eyes, waiting for her cue. Once Jordan had started kissing her, however, they'd been egged on by the crowd. In minutes, they'd been plastered together, arms around each other, making out to an audience.

"Why didn't you say anything when we met again at Marisa's fund-raiser a couple of years ago?"

"Please, I know your type."

"Of course."

She tossed her head, ponytail swinging. "It wasn't important, except for the fact that spring break experience backed up my impression of your reputation since then."

"Naturally."

Her brows drew together again. "Are you humoring me?"

"I'm still processing your bombshell. Our lips have touched."

"Another reason I didn't mention it. We're in-laws. It would make things awkward."

"Or interesting. I've thought that family gatherings could use some spicing up." His lips quirked. "So I knew you in your wilder, younger days, Perini?"

Her naive days—when she was like Danica.

"What went wrong?"

She folded her arms.

"So let me get this straight. Your grudge against me is that I don't remember kissing you?"

"When it was over, you turned away and laughed for the benefit of your friends." As if nothing had happened. As if she didn't matter. Her heart had plummeted. She'd crashed to earth—sort of embarrassed and humiliated. "And then you merged into the crowd."

Her ego had taken a hit back then—only to be run over by Neil a few years later. She had to face it—she sucked at dealing with men.

"Hey—"

"My job here is done," she said, cutting him off and checking her watch.

This time, she was the one to walk away—fading quickly into the crowd. But all the while, she was aware of Jordan's gaze on her back...

Five

Sera gritted her teeth as she made her way to her car in the dark parking lot. It was an older-model domestic sedan that she'd bought used after dealing with a slippery salesman. Slick men—the world was full of them!

She should never have done Angus a favor by coming in to waitress. Her blood still thrummed through her veins from clashing with Jordan Serenghetti. Or rather, she'd clashed while he'd looked underwhelmed—blowing her off as if he were amused by the whole scenario. Typical.

She fumed. She had a bad experience that she'd been nursing as a secret for *years*. And when her big moment had finally arrived and she'd let loose, Jordan's response had been mild. *What was the big deal?*

It all reminded her of…oh, yeah, her confrontation

with Neil about his cheating. Or rather his using her, unwittingly, as the other woman in an affair. Even confronted with the incontrovertible truth, he'd been full of justifications and excuses. *You're special. I meant to tell you.* And her favorite: *It's not what you think.*

Serafina still burned every time she remembered how she'd been taken in by Neil's lies. She'd told Marisa and Dante the cursory details. In fact, she probably shouldn't have divulged anything at all and simply said the relationship had ended. In the aftermath of that debacle, she hadn't wanted anyone to think she still needed protecting and couldn't be trusted to exercise good judgment.

She'd told herself that any woman could have been duped by Neil. He oozed charisma and charm. Just like Jordan Serenghetti.

Oh, Neil had lacked fame, but notoriety would have interfered with his twisted schemes anyway. The press would have made it much harder for him to hide the fact that he had a wife and kid tucked away in Boston. *The rat.*

Do you really know a person if you see only one side of him? Sera had had plenty of time to contemplate that question since breaking up with Neil.

She got behind the wheel and pulled out of the lot for the drive home. She lived in a two-bedroom condo on the opposite side of town that she'd inherited from Marisa. When her cousin had gotten married and moved out, Sera had jumped at the chance to buy the apartment for a very reasonable price. Fortunately, because traffic was light and she knew the route well, she could drive practically on autopilot.

As she started on the main road, Sera replayed the evening. The only reason she'd agreed to help Angus was that she had a whole four consecutive days off from her physical-therapy position. What was one Saturday night helping out a friend and former boss? Plus, she was paying off student loans, so she could use the extra wages and tips from a night moonlighting as a waitress, an aproned superhero saving innocent young women who were easy prey for—

Sera snorted. She should have known it wouldn't be a simple favor. *Of course Jordan would be there.* Saying things she hadn't expected him to say. Looking almost…normal…relatable. She couldn't afford mixed feelings where he was concerned. *Danica isn't my type.* It made her wonder who was—and that was the problem.

Sera flexed her fingers on the steering wheel. The last thing she needed was to be mooning over Jordan Serenghetti. She didn't need to be wondering—mulling—what was on his mind.

Suddenly, she spotted a flurry of movement from the corner of her eye. In an instant, a bear appeared directly in front of her car. Sera sucked in a breath and then jerked hard on the steering wheel to avoid hitting it.

Then everything happened in a blur. Sera bounced around in her seat as the car went off the road in the darkness. She heard and felt tree branches hit the windshield and the car doors. Fear took over, and she hit the brakes hard.

An eternity later—or maybe it was just a couple

of seconds—the car jerked to a stop, and the engine cut out.

Sera sat frozen with shock. *What...?* It had all happened *so fast...*

She threw the emergency break and then blinked at the debris marring her front window. Taking a shaky breath, she leaned her head against the steering wheel. Tremors coursed up her arms from her grip on the wheel.

Great, just great.

At least she hadn't hit the bear.

Could this night get any worse? She wanted to cry but instead gave herself a scolding. After several moments, still shaken, she raised her head and stared into the darkness. It wasn't safe to be a lone woman stranded by the side of the road at night. On top of it, she didn't know where that bear was, but with any luck, she'd managed to frighten him off with their near miss.

Of course, she could use her cell phone to call for help. Dante or another relative would come if she called. Still, she hated being poor, helpless Sera again in the eyes of her family—which was how they would see it.

Suddenly, headlights appeared in her rearview mirror. Sera shook off the touch of fear. It was just someone driving by. Someone who would most likely simply keep on going—because she didn't even have her hazard lights on. Statistically speaking, it was unlikely to be an ax murderer.

But the car slowed down as it passed. Then, a few yards down the road, the driver pulled over.

When the person behind the wheel got out, she immediately recognized Jordan Serenghetti even with only the dim illumination of his flashlight.

Sera suppressed a groan. Not an ax murderer, but someone even more improbable. Jordan. Though she supposed she shouldn't be surprised, since he'd been at the Puck & Shoot, too, and the bar was minutes away.

Unsteadily, she got out of the car, determined to put on a brave front. His appearance just added to her turbulent emotions.

Jordan's face was pulled into an uncharacteristic frown as he approached, looking from her to her car and back again. *He even looked attractive with a scowl.*

"Are you all right?" he asked, for once not displaying his trademark devil-may-care expression.

"Isn't that my line?" How many times had she asked him the same thing during a physical-therapy session? She raised her chin, but with horror, she realized there had been a slight tremor in her voice. *Not all right. Damn it.* She cleared her throat.

He came close, and she'd never seen him appear more serious.

"What are you doing?"

"Checking you for obvious signs of injury. Relax. I'll take it as a good sign that you were able to get out of the car under your own power."

His gaze searched hers in the dim light. "Despite what you think of me, I like to give a hand when I see someone in trouble."

She blinked. "Oh."

"Anything hurt?"

"No." And then she blurted, "What are you doing here?"

Jordan managed to look aggrieved—another new expression for him. "I decided to leave right after you did."

"The fun was gone?" Impossibly, she was challenging him, even though she'd just been in an accident—maybe *because* she'd just been in an accident. She didn't like feeling vulnerable.

"You could say that, but I guess it was good timing—" he gave her a significant look "—because I happened by right after your accident."

"I would have been perfectly fine without your help." No way was Jordan Serenghetti her knight in shining armor.

"Well, judging by your mouth, you're not hurt. And I figure you're going to deny being shaken up. So what happened?"

It irked that he could tell she was rattled. "I swerved to avoid a bear in the road." She grimaced and scanned the woods around them. "In fact, I hope it's not hanging around."

"It's unlikely to view you as a threat." His lips quirked. "I, on the other hand…"

She flushed. Considering she'd just tried to stage a takedown of his womanizing ways back at the bar, she could hardly argue. Next, she expected a critique of her driving skills, but surprisingly it didn't come.

Instead, Jordan examined her car, training his flashlight on the front.

She bit back a gasp as the badly dented front fender was illuminated. And the headlight had been taken out. Her car was a piece of junk, but now she'd have to add automotive repair costs to her budget.

Jordan tucked the flashlight under his arm and pulled out his cell phone.

"What do you think you're doing?"

"Being practical," he responded mildly, walking a few steps away. "I'm getting highway patrol out here."

"You're calling the police?" she said.

His gaze met hers. "So you don't have to. Your insurance may require a police report."

Sera wrapped her arms around herself. The night was warm, but she suddenly felt chilled. She could fume at his take-charge attitude—or grudgingly accept his help, despite what had just happened between them at the Puck & Shoot.

Within minutes, as Jordan continued his inspection of her car, the police showed up. Sera could only conclude there must have been a highway-patrol car in the vicinity.

When the patrolman got out of his car and approached, he paused a moment, and then obviously recognizing Jordan, his expression relaxed. "Hey, you're Jordan Serenghetti."

"Yup."

"Got into a little fender bender tonight?"

"Not me, her."

Sera watched as the police officer's gaze came to rest on her. She gave a jaunty little wave that belied her emotions. So this was what it felt like to play second fiddle to Jordan's star power.

"What happened?" the officer asked, his gaze now on her.

"I swerved to avoid a bear that appeared on the

road." She gestured at her car. "And, well, you can figure out the rest."

The officer rubbed the back of his neck. "Uh-huh."

"She may need paperwork for insurance purposes," Jordan put in.

"Right."

The police officer put up flares while Jordan summoned a tow truck.

When the officer got back to her, she had her driver's license and insurance information ready as another patrol car pulled up.

Again the officer—another middle-aged blond guy—did a double take when he saw Jordan.

The first officer patted his colleague on the shoulder as he went by to his car to fill out the necessary paperwork, and Jordan chatted casually with the new arrival, who obviously couldn't believe his luck at running into a sports celebrity during his shift.

Sera was miserable. The night had gone from bad to worse. She should be slipping between bedcovers right now in soft, worn pajamas. Instead, she was in the middle of a Jordan Serenghetti fan moment.

When the tow truck arrived, the driver slowed his steps as he approached Jordan, and Sera resisted the urge to roll her eyes.

"You're—"

"Jordan Serenghetti," Sera supplied. "Yes, we know."

Jordan's lips twitched. "Don't mind her, she's testy." He shrugged. "You know, accident and all."

The tow truck driver's gaze skimmed over both of them. "Well, at least no one was hurt."

Yet. Yes, she was irritable. Sera waved her hand at Jordan. "He is."

The driver and the police officer still standing nearby both raised their brows.

"Knee surgery," Sera supplied laconically. "I'm sure you two gentlemen have heard about it in the sports news."

Before either man could say anything, Jordan added, "Yeah, and my physical therapist is a badass. I go to bed aching."

The men chuckled, and Sera narrowed her eyes. What had she been thinking about no one being hurt *yet*?

Unfortunately for her, it took another half hour for her car to be towed and the police to be done.

As both officers headed to their cars after the tow truck departed, Jordan turned to her. "I'll drive you."

"Please. The last thing the two of us need is to be in the same moving vehicle together." The police had clearly thought she had a ride with Jordan, though— one they no doubt would have loved to take themselves as his fans. Sera gritted her teeth. "I can use the ride-hailing app on my phone to get a car to pick me up. My apartment is on the other side of town."

"Yeah, you moved into Marisa's old place," Jordan said, ignoring the first part of her reply.

"So you know just how far it is." Sera supposed she shouldn't be surprised that he knew where she lived.

He tossed her a sidelong look. "Great, my place is closer. Let's go."

Wait—what? Had he not heard what she'd said? She was not going to Jordan's place.

As if reading her thoughts, he added, "You're shaken up, and I'm not leaving you alone to be picked up in the dark by a driver you don't even know."

"As opposed to you? Because you're the safer bet? And anyway, chivalry is dead."

"So angelic and yet so cynical," Jordan murmured.

"With good reason!"

"I'll get you a car from my place once I'm convinced you're all right."

It was hard to be mad at someone when you owed them a favor.

And the last person she wanted to be indebted to for help was Jordan Serenghetti.

Somehow, she was going to live down tonight's debacle. Somehow, she was going to get through weeks of physical therapy with Jordan. Her mind ping-ponged, hit by a gamut of emotions as she stepped into Jordan's apartment.

His place had the ambience of an athlete…a jock… a celebrity…a sports star living there. But shockingly, Sera couldn't sniff *playboy* in the air as she paused next to the elevator that had just deposited them in his penthouse. Everything was modern, pristine and orderly. White walls, chocolate upholstery and stainless-steel appliances. It was far from the messy fraternity house existence that she'd been expecting.

And then, because Jordan was watching her as they stood just inside his apartment, she said, "So this is how the other half lives."

"It's not that fancy."

Her gaze drifted toward the back of his apartment.

"Your Viking range alone must have cost thousands of dollars. And I'm guessing you don't even really cook."

"No, but my mother does. So she has expectations."

The apartment was dim and quiet...and Jordan was standing too close. So much so that she picked up on the scent that she had started to identify as uniquely his.

As a result of their physical-therapy sessions, she was well-acquainted with the reasons why *some* women found him attractive. He was all toned and sculpted muscle—with a lean, hard jaw and wicked glint in his green eyes. Even injured, he exuded a powerful magnetism. This close, she had to lift her head to make eye contact, making her even more aware of just how *male* he was. Now that he was out of his milieu— a sports bar—she could momentarily forget why she didn't like him. *Almost.*

They stared at each other in the dim light.

The corner of his mouth lifted. "Lost for words?"

"I've spent them all."

"Yeah, I know."

All that remained unsaid hung between them.

"Come on in," he said.

"I thought I was getting a car."

"In a sec." He regarded her thoughtfully. "But first you look like you could use a shoulder to lean on."

"Not yours." To her horror, however, her voice wasn't as strong and steady as she would have liked. The hour was late, she was tired and she'd had one roller coaster of a day. Suddenly, it was all catching up to her and was just too much. Right now, she wanted to be in fluffy socks and battered sweats and holding a cup of herbal tea. Not dealing with the complexities of her relationship with Jordan. No, wait—they didn't have a *relationship*.

Jordan searched her face with an annoyingly penetrating gaze. "Are you okay?"

"Fine." Could that high-pitched voice possibly be hers? But fortunately, he hadn't brought up their conversation at the Puck & Shoot.

"Sera."

She felt as if she were drowning.

"Aw, hell," Jordan said.

In the next instant, he'd folded her into his arms, smoothing his hands down her back as he tucked her head under his chin.

She stiffened. "You're the last person—"

"I know."

"I don't even like you. You are irritating and rude and—"

"—ridiculous?"

"This is a delayed reaction," she sniffed, relaxing into his embrace.

"Understandable."

"If you breathe a word about this to anyone, Serenghetti…"

"Not likely. Your reputation is safe with me."

"Great."

She was more shaken up by her accident than she'd thought. More shaken up by *everything*.

He stroked his hand up and down her back, lulling her. She leaned into him. They stayed that way as time ticked by for she couldn't say how long.

It was quiet, and the lights of Welsdale twinkled outside.

Slowly, though, as she regained steadiness, comfort gave way to something else. She became aware of subtle changes. Jordan's breathing deepened, and hers grew shallower and more rapid.

He shifted, dipping his head, and his lips grazed her temple.

She lifted her head and met his gaze. "So these are the famous Jordan Serenghetti moves these days? A hug?"

Their faces were inches apart, and she remained pressed against him—his long, lean form imprinting her, making her *feel*.

"How am I doing?"

She lifted her shoulders. "Do you usually look for a rating?"

"You still have a smart mouth, Perini," he muttered.

"Weaponized? And you're going to disarm me, I bet," she replied tartly.

He bent toward her and muttered, "Worth risking serious injury for."

"I dare you." She tossed out the words carelessly, but she was all taut awareness because she'd never seen Jordan this focused and intent.

"You know that kiss…"

Her brows drew together. "What about it?"

"Since I don't remember it, I'm curious."

She sucked in a breath and then warned, "Since there's no audience to cheer you on this time, why bother?"

He pressed the pad of his thumb against her bottom lip. "Such a loaded question. Let's find out."

And just like that, he kissed her.

She tried for nonchalance. Still, his mouth was lazy and sensual, coaxing hers into a slow dance.

Eventually, the kiss took on a life of its own. In fact, Sera wasn't sure what possessed her. The need to tangle with a player again—and this time be the one who came out ahead? Perhaps a desire to prove that she was older and wiser and not so green—and therefore wouldn't be hurt? She couldn't say—and maybe didn't want to examine the issue too closely.

Jordan cupped the sides of her face, his fingers tunneling into her hair, and held her steady. His mouth was warm, searching...confident.

He swept his tongue around hers, and she met him, every part of her responding. She gripped his shirt, pulling him in, and he made a low sound in his throat.

She'd wondered over the years whether her memory of their kiss had been dulled by time. Had it really been that good? Not that she'd been looking for a repeat lately, she told herself. It had just been idle curiosity sparked by seeing Jordan again. And since he'd been so annoying and able to bring out her snarky best, she'd assumed her recollection was off.

Wrong, so wrong.

Every part of her came to life, sensitized to his touch, his scent, his taste. And there was no lazy humor to Jordan now. Instead, everything about him said he wanted to strip off her waitress clothes so they could both find bliss...

When the kiss broke off, he trailed his lips across

her jaw, and she tilted her head so that he could continue the path down the side of her neck. His hand came up to cup her breast, and she strained against him, wanting more, a sound of pleasure escaping her lips.

He brought his mouth to hers again, and his leg wedged between her thighs. She skimmed her hands along his back, feeling the ripped muscles move under her caress.

Jordan's scent enveloped her—the one she'd started to know so well and had fought against. But his casual devil-may-care persona was stripped away, and all he seemed to care about was getting closer to her, exploring the attraction that she'd often dismissed as just smooth moves on his part.

He tugged her T-shirt from the waistband of her skirt as their kiss took on a new urgency. Pushing aside her bra, he found her breast with his hand and palmed it tenderly.

She moved against him, feeling the friction of his jeans straining to hold back his arousal, and he broke off the kiss on a curse.

Lifting her shirt, he looked down as he stroked her breast, his chest rising and falling with awareness.

She glanced down, too, and watched him caress her, her excitement growing.

"So beautiful," he muttered. "Perfect."

He rested his forehead against hers—and their breath mingled, short and deep and fast. "Let me touch you."

Her brain foggy with desire, she didn't understand for a moment, until she felt his hand slide under her skirt. Pushing aside her panties, he began gently exploring her.

Sera's head fell back, her eyes closing.

"So good," Jordan murmured in a voice she didn't recognize. "Ah, Angel, let me in."

She let him stroke her, building the heat inside her. She shifted to give him better access, and he built a rhythm that she enjoyed…until he pressed his thumb against her and she splintered, her world fracturing, filling with their labored breaths and the scent of Jordan all around her.

They stood that way for moments, and Sera slowly came down to earth, her breath slowing.

What was she doing?

With a remaining bit of sanity, she pulled back, and he loosened his hold. Then she laid her hand on his chest as if to underscore the distance she needed. She felt the strong, steady beat of his heart, reminding her of the sexual thrum between them.

He didn't move. His jaw firm, he seemed carved out of stone, his face stamped with unfulfilled sexual desire in the dim illumination.

She felt like a heel—an uncomfortable and new feeling where Jordan was considered. Still, they couldn't, they shouldn't. "This is so wrong. We—"

"Angel—"

"We shouldn't have done that."

And then she ran. Grabbing the purse that she'd come in with, she turned and stabbed the button for the elevator.

"Sera—"

She nearly gasped with relief when the door slid right open and Jordan made no move to stop her.

As the elevator door closed, she called hurriedly over her shoulder, "I'll summon a cab downstairs with my phone."

Six

Jordan came awake. The bedsheets were a tangled mess around him because he'd had a restless night.

Sera. The one-word answer for why he'd been edgy.

He'd dreamed about her after she'd left in a hurry. At least in sleep, he'd gotten a chance to indulge many of his fantasies from the past couple months. He'd guided her and learned her pleasure points with his hands and mouth. He'd whispered all the indecent things he wanted to do with her, and she hadn't blinked. But unfortunately, none of it had been real. In real life, Sera had hurried out of his apartment.

He was still wrapping his mind around all the revelations from last night. Their kiss had been fantastic enough to fuel fantasies all night long. He'd had a hunch they'd be combustible together, and he'd been proven right. More than right. Things had escalated, and if Sera hadn't broken things off, he had his doubts they would have bothered making it from the entry to his bed. She'd been soft and curvy and responsive, just like he'd imagined. *Better than he'd imagined.* She had the softest skin he'd ever caressed.

Sera was soft despite her seemingly hard shell. Who knew?

And how the hell could he have forgotten someone as hot and memorable as Serafina Perini? He racked his brain for memories from eight years ago. Could he really have been as much of a jerk as she'd made him out to be?

Sera had been pissed off at being so easily consigned to oblivion. No question about it.

The only answer was that he'd been young and stupid and immature. Flush with the first victories of a burgeoning hockey career that had put his sickly childhood behind him, and intent on enjoying his new status and image as a chick magnet and sports stud.

Yup. That explanation would go over well with Sera.

She'd have to deal with him, though, at their next therapy session—and to make matters more complicated, she was now driving his car. After Sera had departed in a rush last night, he'd called downstairs and told Donnie at the security desk to offer her the second set of keys to his sedan. She'd need a car until her beaten-up wreck got fixed, and Jordan would be fine driving his pickup in the meantime. Fortunately, Donnie had later reported that Sera had reluctantly taken up the offer.

Jordan smiled over the irony as he stared at the ceiling. His car had been the fastest and easiest way for her to escape from him.

After a moment, he tossed the covers off and headed to the shower. He needed to clear his head and brainstorm a way out of this bind. *What the hell was he supposed to say to her at their next physical therapy session?*

And then there was the other problem he'd been meaning to get to ever since his last conversation with his mother. He bit back a grimace and figured he was overdue for trying to sort out a different Serenghetti family tangle. Plus, it would take his mind off Sera.

An hour later, after downing a quick breakfast, he headed to his parents' house on the outskirts of Welsdale.

He found his father in an armchair, remote in hand, in the large living room that ran most of the width of the back of the house.

"Hi, Dad. Where's Mom?"

Serg Serenghetti looked up grumpily. "At work. The cleaning service just left."

"Yeah, I know. Conveniently, they let me in as they headed out." Jordan smiled gamely. "So it's just us guys, then."

His father glanced at him from under bushy brows. Then he clicked the remote to change the channel from golf to a commercial.

"What are you going to watch?"

"One of those home-improvement shows your generation loves." He guffawed. "As if any of these TV performers really knows the biz."

"Right." Jordan settled onto the sofa next to his father's armchair.

Serg waved the remote. "If any of my children was interested, you'd be helping Serenghetti Construction with a television show."

"Try Rick. He's got the Hollywood ties these days." Jordan looked around. "Quiet here."

"If your mother was home, she'd just be fussing." Serg turned off the TV. "Now it's quiet."

Jordan shook his head bemusedly. His parents' marriage had lasted decades, producing four kids and now grandkids, while riding the ups and downs of Serenghetti Construction. His parents had met when his mother had been a front-desk clerk at a hotel in Tuscany, and Serg had been on his way to visit extended family north of Venice. So the whole feed-and-shelter hospitality biz was in his mother's blood, and the latest incarnation of that was her cooking show. Until recently, his father had handled the sheltering part with his construction business, while his mother was all about sustenance.

Except that had all gotten upended lately. "So what's got you down?"

"If you spent your days out of a job, sitting here watching TV, you'd be surly, too."

"Right."

Serg lowered his brows. "Come to think of it, that's not too far off from where you are."

Jordan shifted in his seat, because it hadn't occurred to him before now that he and his father might have something more in common these days than sharing a passing family resemblance. An extended convalescence had prevented them both from returning to their old lives. In his father's case, permanently. And in his... Chills ran up Jordan's arms.

He'd thought that his days being sick and bedridden were well past him. But being sidelined with his injury brought back the old feelings of helplessness.

His father was nearing seventy. Not young, but not really old, either. Jordan wondered where he'd be at that age. Certainly not playing hockey, but what would his second act be? At least, he had some plans for what to do with his earnings as long as his injury didn't get in the way.

"You need a second act," he said into the void.

Serg grumbled and shifted. "Your mother doesn't like to share the limelight."

Jordan smiled slightly. "Yeah, I heard. You'd like a segment on Mom's show."

"The audience loved me when I did a special guest spot suggesting wine pairings."

"You should revel in Mom's success," Jordan went on. "But I get it. She's at the top of her game, and you're at a crossroads."

"Since when are you the family psychologist?"

Jordan chuckled. "Yeah, I know. It's a dirty job, but someone in this family has to do it, and I did well running interference for Cole and Marisa."

Serg lowered his chin and peered over at him. "Jordan, your sport is hockey, not football."

"Okay, fair enough. So...back to you and Mom."

"We're out of your league. Don't try to run interference."

"Right." The message was clear, but he had one of

his own. "But maybe instead of wanting a piece of Mom's success, you should develop your own game."

Every once in a while, Sera thought it was a good idea to have Sunday dinner at her mother's house. Today was not one of those days.

The simple three-bedroom shingle house with a postage-stamp lawn stood on a tidy side street in East Gannon. Its no-frills white appliances were a world away from the high-end stainless steel in Jordan's sleek, modern penthouse. Here, it was all open bookshelves displaying books, mementos and family photos—not unobtrusive panels concealing high-end electronics, as well as its owner's secrets.

And the contrasts didn't end there. Jordan's place was forward-looking, with very little evidence of the past, as far as she could tell. Her mother's place held a hint of nostalgia—now that the kids had grown and flown the coop—and sadness since Sera's father's death from a heart attack a few years ago. His passing had been the wake-up call that Sera had needed to get on with her life and go back to school for a physical-therapy degree.

At the dinner table, Sera twirled some spaghetti onto her fork. Her mother was an excellent cook, and tonight's chicken parmigiana and spaghetti with tomato sauce was no exception. Ever since her mother had been widowed, Sera and Dante had made it a point to visit regularly. They knew their mother appreciated the companionship.

"I heard you had a car accident." Her mother's brow was furrowed with worry.

Sera cleared her fork and started twirling it again because she'd accidentally put on too much spaghetti. Good thing she hadn't had a mouthful already. On the other hand, maybe she should have welcomed an excuse not to talk… "How did you find out?"

"Dante's friend Jeff happened to be at the auto shop earlier today. He overheard the employee there on the phone with you, taking down your personal information to fix your car." Her mother tossed her an arch look across the dining-room table. "There aren't many women running around with the name Serafina Perini."

For the umpteenth time, Sera rued having a unique name. And she sometimes forgot what a small town Welsdale could be. Still, she was lucky that the most popular local auto body shop had Sunday hours because she'd been able to call and get a status report about when she might get her car back. Unfortunately, the news hadn't been encouraging, and it looked like she was stuck driving Jordan's wheels for a while. Too bad every time she climbed into the car, she was unable to shake his scent.

She'd been surprised when the guy at the security desk in Jordan's building had offered her car keys on Jordan's instructions, but after hesitating a moment, she'd chosen the path of least resistance—one that would solve her immediate problems, whatever the longer-term consequences. She now owed Jordan a favor when she should have been mad at him—and then there was the little complication about what else had happened that evening at his place…

"I assume you got a rental car until yours is fixed,"

her mother observed, "and that's how you got here today."

"Yes, I have temporary wheels." Jordan Serenghetti's.

"Are you okay?" her mother asked.

She schooled her expression with the help of her reflection in the china closet's glass door. "Fine, Mom."

"Why didn't you tell me about your accident?"

"I just did." Her mother would be even more shocked if she knew how Sera had wound up in Jordan Serenghetti's arms in the aftermath of her fender bender.

"You know what I mean. The mothers are always the last to know." Rosana sighed. "I bet your cousin Marisa would have told your aunt right away."

Her mother knew how to play the guilt card... And if there was one thing that Sera had grown up hearing about ad nauseam, it was the close relationship that Aunt Donna had with her cousin Marisa. Never mind that Aunt Donna had raised her only child as a single mother, making her and Marisa a family of two, relying on each other. Rosana Perini looked up to her older sister, even as she took her sibling's life as a cautionary tale. Ever since Donna had been left pregnant and alone by a professional minor-league baseball player who'd died unexpectedly soon after, Rosana had worried about her. But she'd been thrilled when her older sister had finally found love again with Ted Casale.

"Do you want me to ask Dante to go down to the auto body shop?"

"No. I'm capable of handling my own car repairs."

"Do you need some money?"

Sera deployed a tight smile. "No, I can handle it, Mom."

The last thing Sera wanted was for her family to think they needed to come to her aid. She'd spent most of her twentysomething years trying to shed the image of poor Sera who needed rescuing and protecting.

"Thank goodness you got home okay." Her mother frowned again. "You should have called me."

If only her mother knew that she hadn't gone directly home but had been sidetracked at Jordan's place. A detour that had risked turning into an all-night change of direction, if she hadn't put the brakes on their intimate encounter. Then, to cover her bases, she volunteered, "I was lucky that Jordan Serenghetti happened to be driving by. I got a lift."

Not straight home. But her mother didn't need to know that. Sera had been offering up information on a strictly as-necessary basis to her family for years. But it wouldn't do if word somehow got back to her mother that Jordan had been at the scene of the accident and Sera hadn't mentioned it. Dodging suspicion—that was what she'd been doing ever since she'd been a rebellious teenager cutting the occasional high-school class to hang out with friends.

Rosana Perini shot her a disapproving look. "Another reason I worry about you living alone. Who'd know for hours if you didn't make it home?"

Exactly. Who'd know she'd almost spent last night at Jordan's place? She couldn't believe how quickly things had gotten hot and heavy. She'd been thinking all day about it, in fact. *Reliving the highlights.* He'd brought her to satisfaction right there in his foyer. Sera felt her face flame and hoped her mother didn't notice.

Jordan's power to charm and seduce was beyond her understanding. The realization had unnerved her and sent her hightailing it out of his apartment.

She'd already resolved to treat last night as an aberration never to be repeated. She'd had her guard down and had been running on emotion from an evening capped off by having her car banged up. *Yup, that was her story, and she was sticking to it.* She just needed to convince Jordan to treat last night as if it had never happened and swear him to silence about the whole comforting-embrace-leading-to-fringe-benefits thing.

"It was another story when you and Marisa were roommates," Rosana Perini continued, jerking Sera back to the present, "but now you've got no one nearby."

Except for Jordan. Sera kept her tone light. "I bought Marisa's condo when she got married. I've still got the protective family aura that she left behind."

Her mother heaved a sigh. "You were always sassy, unlike your brother."

"I know. Dante is an angel. I guess you just got the names wrong, Mom."

"Speaking of Dante, he has a new job."

"Yes, I know, he told me." How could she forget? Her brother's new employment was what had gotten her into her current fix. Her gig as Jordan's physical therapist meant she'd have to spend time again and again with the in-law she'd been intimate with.

The doorbell sounded, and her mother got up. "I wonder who that is."

Moments later, Sera heard voices, and then her brother followed her mother into the room.

"Dante, this is a wonderful surprise," her mother said. "We were just talking about you."

Dante filched a piece of bread from the table and bit into it.

Rosana's face was wreathed in smiles as she headed for the kitchen. "I'll set another plate and heat up some more food. I always make extra."

Dante winked at Sera and swallowed. "And today, your just-in-case habit paid off. Thanks, Mom."

As their mother disappeared, Sera regarded her brother. "You made her happy."

"Anything for Mom." Dante took a seat opposite her, polishing off the last of his bread in the process. "I didn't know you were here. Your car wasn't out front."

"It's there," Sera mumbled. "I parked around the corner."

Dante snagged a piece of cheese from an appetizer plate. "Why would you do that?"

Sera sighed. This was why she was careful around her family. It was always lots of questions—with a subtext of questioning her judgment. And then, because she figured Dante would find out anyway, Sera said, "I got into a little fender bender last night, so I'm driving Jordan Serenghetti's car."

Dante stopped and swallowed. "Whoa, hold up. I'm still processing the cause and effect. How do you go from a little fender bender to driving the Razors' top gun's fancy wheels?" Her brother grinned. "That's some fast work, sis. I'm employed by the Razors organization, and I haven't even had a chance to grab a beer with Jordan yet."

"Hilarious, Dante." She cast a quick look at the kitchen to make sure their mother wasn't coming back. "Jordan drove by right after the accident."

"Just happened to drive by, huh?"

"Yes," she said, holding her brother's gaze but nevertheless lowering her voice. If she couldn't convince Dante there wasn't the scent of a juicy story here, she was doomed with everyone else. "After my car was towed, Jordan lent me his. It was generous of him."

Dante nodded. "Generous."

Sera tilted her head. "What's the matter with you? Have you turned into a parrot?"

Her brother coughed. "Just trying to understand the facts."

Sera smiled brightly. "Well, there you have it. End of story."

"I thought the goal here was to get Jordan Serenghetti feeling indebted to the Perinis, not the other way around," her brother teased.

Tell me about it.

"By the way, how's it going with my favorite hockey player?"

"Who?" she joked.

Dante bit off a laugh. "Jordan Serenghetti, of course."

Sera debated how to answer. Obviously, *I nearly slept with him* was not the right choice. "He's visiting the clinic weekly and…coming along nicely."

"And you're still his physical therapist?" her brother asked gingerly.

Therapist, in-law, hookup—did the label really matter? "Yup."

Dante relaxed and sat back in his chair. "I knew I could count on you, Sera."

"I didn't say he'd be able to start the season. We're still weeks away from any medical clearance." She took a bite of her chicken parmigiana.

Dante nodded. "But you're helping me get off on the right foot at the office. I've dropped the information into key conversations that my sister is Jordan Serenghetti's physical therapist."

"Yup, you owe me one." Wouldn't Rosana Perini be surprised to know that Sera was helping Dante instead of the other way around? "Don't worry, I'll keep your dirty little secret from Mom. The halo will stay intact."

"You're priceless, sis."

"It's a big favor." Probably the biggest that Dante had ever asked of her, come to think of it. All her instincts had told her to dump Jordan as a client as soon as possible—he was too much for her to handle on every level, and she'd been miserable at keeping it professional—but she was sticking it out for her brother's sake.

"Oh, come on, Jordan Serenghetti isn't that bad. I'll bet there are plenty of hockey fans in the ranks of physical therapists who'd love to have him as a client."

"I'm not one of them." She just planned to survive the coming couple of months or so at her job—somehow—and be done. Before anyone discovered *her* dirty little secret—which she'd make Jordan swear to take to the grave.

Seven

She could do this. Sera sucked in a breath as she prepared to face Jordan Serenghetti again for the first time since *that night*. It was already Wednesday afternoon and time for their next therapy session. Somehow, she had to do an impossible balancing act between remaining professional and having a frank conversation that addressed moving forward from Saturday's events.

If their families caught even a whiff of this… *situation*, that there was more to it than Jordan just lending her his car, it would be like a powder keg exploding. She'd never hear the end of it, never live it down. Everyone would look at her and Jordan and *know*.

She had to make the potential repercussions clear to Jordan—if he didn't understand them already. *And* she also had to put the genie back in the bottle regarding what happened eight years ago—all in the hour or so they had for their therapy session.

She rolled her eyes. *She could do this.* How hard could it be? She was dealing with a love 'em and leave 'em type who tossed baggage overboard and bailed… He should have no trouble agreeing to keep things under wraps, right?

But yesterday's delivery from the florist, arranged by Jordan, had made her think she had her work cut out for her.

And unfortunately, she was still driving his car—inhaling his scent and touching his belongings. She told herself that was the reason she couldn't get him out of her mind. And she had to concede it had been a nice thing to do to lend her his ride—a *very expensive* luxury sedan tricked out with leather upholstery and all the latest gadgets that made her beat-up secondhand car look like a horse and buggy. Her own vehicle continued to be in the shop for repairs, and she'd had to make time-consuming calls to her insurance company.

As she stepped into the exam room at Astra Therapeutics, her gaze came to rest on Jordan leaning against the treatment table. Having no need for crutches anymore, he looked even more formidable.

He was dressed in a T-shirt and jeans. Really, what the man could do to a pair of jeans—let alone underwear—was sinful. And he was looking at her as if she were a pint of his favorite ice cream and he was a spoon.

Being this close to him for the first time after Saturday night caused memories to flood back. Her pulse picked up, and she fought the sudden visceral urge to fit back into his arms and pick up where they'd left off. *Have mercy.* This was going to be even harder than she'd thought.

"Hello, sunshine."

"We're here for your rehab." She set down her clipboard. Staying businesslike helped her not lose her mind. She planned to address their never-to-be-repeated Saturday night. *Just not quite yet.* She needed to work up to it and then make it short and sweet.

He looked deep into her eyes. "I missed you after you left."

So much for steering him in a different direction. "Well, I'm here now."

"How's my car working out for you?"

"Fine." And that was the problem. She'd felt enveloped by him for the past four days.

He took her hand, surprising her, and ran his thumb over the back of her palm.

She swallowed. "What happens in the penthouse stays in the penthouse."

He stopped and gazed at her.

She could see herself daydreaming about his changeable green eyes. The whimsical thought passed through her head before she opened her mouth and got back to her script. "You and I are taking what happened on Saturday night to our graves."

Jordan's lips twitched. "The car accident?"

"You know what I mean." She extracted her hand from his because unnecessary touching was a no-no. "The ban includes flowers like those that arrived yesterday." The bouquet had been delivered after she'd gotten home. A lovely bouquet of lilies and… "Achillea Angel's Breath."

Jordan smiled. "I asked the florist for a flower with *angel* in the name."

"Of course."

"You mean a long line of boyfriends has been sending them to you?"

"No, you're the first." *Rats.* Most guys went for the familiar and easy—roses, carnations. She didn't want to give him bonus points for being imaginative. "The flowers were…lovely, but I'm glad you didn't send them to me at work."

Jordan winked. "I'm not going to blow your cover."

"Right." And getting back to the point: "Just erase Saturday night from your mind. Treat it as if it never happened."

Jordan looked amused. "You're asking to rewind the clock. I don't think I can un-remember how soft your skin is, the way you feel in my arms, how you respond to my touch."

She ignored the flutter of awareness at his words. "Really? You can forget eight years ago, but you can't delete last Saturday?"

"Ouch."

She folded her arms. "Save it for when you're doing leg presses."

Jordan sobered. "I'm sorry I came off as a jerk when we first met years ago."

Sera blinked because an apology wasn't what she was expecting. Still, she couldn't let him think it mattered all that much to her, so she waved a hand dismissively. "Please. The only reason I brought it up was because I was annoyed by your smooth-player ways."

Jordan twisted his lips wryly. "The truth is that I've gotten used to laughing off fans' attention or giving them a brief brush with fame and then moving on."

"And those were the moves you were showing Danica at the Puck & Shoot?"

He tilted his head. "As I said, it's easy to fall back on some safe maneuvers."

"So eight years ago, I might have been just another fan coming on to you?" she persisted.

Jordan looked pained. "Okay, that may have been my ego talking."

She dropped her hands. "Exactly."

Jordan held up his hands. "Hey, I'm trying for some honesty here, even if I can't make amends."

Sera lowered her shoulders and sighed. Because, yeah, she'd thought of him as a jerk, but he'd made her look at things from a different perspective. And really, wasn't it best that she accept his explanation and they drop the whole subject—so they could move on as she wanted to?

"So where do we go from here?" Jordan asked, seemingly reading her thoughts.

She pasted a bright smile on her face. "We get started on your physical therapy for the day."

He regarded her thoughtfully for a moment, and Sera held her ground.

"If that's the way you want to play it," he said finally.

"Play is not what I had in mind." Then, seeking a distraction, she concentrated on her clipboard, focusing on her notes and flipping through his paperwork. As if she needed reminding about his file and all the details weren't carved in her memory. Just like Saturday night...

On the fifth page, though, something that she'd initially skimmed over caught her attention. For the question on prior hospitalizations, Jordan had marked *yes* and jokingly written *Too many to mention*.

Hmm. Sera looked over at him. "This was not the first time you've had surgery."

"I'm a professional athlete. What do you think?"

"I think you're familiar with doctors, even if I'm your first physical therapist."

He flashed a brief smile. "I've been giving my mother trouble from day one. Literally. I had a collapsed lung as a newborn. I had some respiratory issues because I inhaled meconium."

She blinked in surprise because this information didn't fit the image she had of Jordan Serenghetti. Cool...invincible.

"And to top it off—" he started counting on his fingers "—a broken arm at age eight, pneumonia at age ten—or wait, was that eleven? And a ruptured appendix at fourteen. I was also in and out of the ER for more minor stuff like an ear infection and a sprained wrist."

"Wonderful."

"Memorable. Just ask the staff at Children's Hospital."

"I'm sure it was for them and you."

He grinned.

Sera felt herself softening and cleared her throat. "Let's get to work."

Jordan followed her from the treatment room to the gym, where they worked on normalizing his gait and improving strength with step exercises and leg presses, among other repetitions. More than a month past surgery, he was regaining mobility.

"So how am I doing?" he asked as they were wrapping up. "Think I'll be able to rejoin the team in the fall?"

Sera tilted her head and paused because, despite his casual tone, she knew the answer mattered to him—a lot. "Mmm, that's a question for your doctor. You're recovering nicely, but there's always some unpredictability post-op. And you're expecting your knee to perform at a high level in professional hockey."

Jordan shrugged. "The PRP therapy that my doctor is doing is helping, too."

"Good. Injections can help speed up recovery." She regarded him, and then offered, "You'll get there eventually. Does it matter when? The last thing you want to do is exacerbate an injury or sustain another tear by getting back on the ice too soon."

"I have some endorsement deals up for negotiation, and my contract with the Razors is coming up for renewal in the next few months. There's a lot on the table."

Oh. Now he told her. Talk about pressure. Not only did Dante need Jordan on the ice—he was a big draw for the fans, obviously—but now there were other deadlines. For a big star like Jordan, his contract and endorsements would be everything.

She'd heard stories about his lucrative investments in business ventures, but still, she was sure that continuing to play hockey was integral to his plans. She knew about other sports celebrities who had gone on to invest in everything from franchises to restaurants to car dealerships, after playing as long as possible.

"Thanks for sharing," she quipped.

Within the four walls of Astra Therapeutics, she'd almost forgotten what a different life he led from the one she did. It was about big money and celebrity and high stakes. Jordan's physical prowess and athleticism had landed him at the pinnacle of professional sports.

"Have dinner with me," he offered, "and I'll tell you all about it. There's a new place in town I've been meaning to try." He shrugged. "But, you know, the knee injury put me off my game."

"Another hockey pub? Angus will be jealous," she parried before getting serious, because she needed to drive this point home. "And we're not dating—remember? Saturday night was a never-to-be-repeated blip on the radar."

"It's not a date. It's friends having dinner. And no, I have someplace a little more sophisticated in mind."

Sera fought the little prick of awareness at his words. He was a master of the segue. "That was smoothly done."

Just like the other night. She'd been replaying the feel of his hands moving over her…again and again. *No…just no.* She wouldn't let herself go there. She was putting Saturday night into a tidy little box and sealing it tight. She took a deep breath. "We're not even friends." *Are we?*

"Okay, in-laws dining out," he responded, but the

gleam in his eyes said he recognized she hadn't said no yet.

"We've got nothing to talk about."

"Sure we do." He consulted his watch. "We've talked our way through this therapy appointment. Time flies."

She looked heavenward. Were all the Serenghettis this stubborn?

"There's plenty to discuss. The latest news from our joint family for one," he said, counting on the fingers of his hand again. "And your aversion to hockey and wariness around men."

Around him. "I have nothing against hockey."

"What about men?"

She sighed. "I'm not allergic to men. Saturday night should have put that notion to rest."

He lifted the corner of his mouth. "Yeah."

She took another deep breath. "Obviously, physical therapy isn't the only type you need. We need to add mindfulness because you have to learn to live in the present and stop cycling back to the past."

"I am living in the moment. And aren't you the one caught in a loop about being burned in the past?"

Back to that, were they? Still, she knew Jordan was only guessing if he was referring to anything beyond their kiss on a beach. There was no way he could know about Neil.

"I want to prove you wrong about me."

She was suspicious, cautious…curious. "Why?"

Jordan gave a small smile. "You're funny and smart. You're a hard worker who went back to school to earn her degree while putting up with smart alecks like me at the Puck & Shoot. You're caring. You trained for a profession that makes a difference in people's lives."

She started to melt and then straightened her spine. Still, she couldn't help asking, "Smart alecks? How about glib lotharios?"

He leaned forward, his look intensifying. "I know I have a reputation, but the other night between us was special. I've never felt a connection that fast with a woman before."

"Because I'm good with a comeback?"

"Angel with a smart mouth, yeah. You're one of a kind."

How many times had she wanted to be special and valued for herself? And she especially didn't want to be known as Sera who needed to be protected—as her family saw her. Still, she had to keep these sessions focused on business—she had her work reputation to think about, even if Bernice was the kind of boss to appreciate a good-looking guy. "I'm a therapist, and you're my client. We have to keep this professional."

"We are. I've been doing the homework that you've assigned."

Sera nearly threw up her hands. He was persistent and had a counterargument for everything.

"I hear that you box," Jordan teased. "I'd ask you to meet me for a date at Jimmy's Boxing Gym so we can hit the punching bags together. It's one of my regular haunts but—" he nodded at his knee with an apologetic expression "—I doubt I'm up to that kind of exercise yet."

"Let's take a rain check, then," she said, dodging

the invitation before glancing at the clock on the wall. "I'm about to be late for my next appointment."

Jordan looked at her as if he saw right through her.

She wished she could take that rain check for their therapy sessions. Because if Jordan kept on with the charm offensive, it was going to be hard to keep up her walls against him…

By the next week's session on Wednesday afternoon, as he waited for Sera's arrival, Jordan had realized he needed a plan B. The problem was he'd so rarely had to resort to a backup strategy where women were concerned, he wasn't even sure what plan B was. Except that he needed one.

Ever since their fateful Saturday night encounter, he couldn't get Sera out of his mind. Her scent lingered, her touch tantalized, her taste made him yearn for more. Sometimes a great memory was a curse. He must have been an ignoramus eight years ago.

The direct approach—an invitation to dinner—hadn't worked with Sera. She wasn't biting, so he needed to sweeten the offer for her. How? Couldn't Cole and Marisa invite some family over for the baby's sleeping-through-the-night celebration or something? He'd debated his options, had searched his brain during interminable repetitions of his physical-therapy routine at home—when all he could think about was her—and had finally come up with a scenario that involved recruiting his mother.

Needing help from his mother to score a date was as low as he'd ever gone. Frankly, it was embarrassing and humbling…and all part of the new territory he was in with Sera.

When Sera entered the treatment room, her expression was all business. Still, she looked fresh and perky and delicious. He now knew she responded to him as no other woman ever had. She was attuned to him on a level he'd never experienced before. So it made it impossible to even pay lip service to her ridiculous plan to forget that Saturday night ever happened.

"Nice move leaving my car keys with the security desk in my building," he observed.

She swept her hair off her shoulder. "Thank you again for the loan of a set of wheels. My car is out of the shop."

"Congratulations. But I thought I'd at least find some memento of your stay." He shrugged. "You know, a forgotten lip balm or a pair of sunglasses. Or at least your lingering scent on the upholstery."

"I wasn't able to do a complete makeover in a few days," she deadpanned right back. "Your imprint was hard to eradicate."

He loved her sass. "But you tried?"

"I'm sure you'd like to be considered unforgettable."

"I'll settle for immortality," he teased.

She scrolled on the tablet she'd brought to their session this time instead of a clipboard with paperwork.

He eyed her. "I've got a request."

She looked up. "I give you points for being direct."

Jordan laughed as he leaned against the treatment table. If Sera wanted to pretend their close encounter hadn't happened or was an anomaly, then he was willing to play any of the limited cards he had left. "I'd like you to appear on my mother's cooking show."

Sera's eyes widened. "What? You can't be serious."

He shrugged. "Consider it a thank-you for the use of my car."

"Sneaky." She took a deep breath. "Anyway, Marisa may have appeared on the program once, but it's not for me. I've caught your mother's show a few times on television, and I consider it a spectator sport."

"My mother's station is under new management. Mom is worried about being canceled and wants to make a good impression. And I'm trying to help her out by coming up with some ideas."

"Why doesn't she just switch to online? She can go viral." Nevertheless Sera contemplated him thoughtfully. "Still, it's nice of you to try to help her."

"I was an Eagle Scout. Good deeds are my forte."

"Are you sure you want to involve your mother? Who knows what I might tell her?"

He smiled lazily. "That's the point. You'll be on the show, so I'll be on my best behavior…because you'll be doing me a kindness."

"You've thought of everything," she remarked drily.

"And it'll be a good show," he pressed. "Just what my mother needs right now."

"How do you know I'd be appropriate? I might burn the calzones."

"C'mon, you bring homemade dishes to the office, and your coworkers praise your cooking." He'd found a bargaining chip in her baked ziti.

"Remind me to tell them not to be so loose-lipped,"

Sera grumbled, nevertheless looking flattered. "No good deed goes unpunished."

Jordan snapped his fingers as an idea hit. "You might teach me how to cook. There's no format yet, but the audience would eat up a show about a pro hockey player bumbling his way through the kitchen."

"Well, somehow I doubt any acting would be involved on your part. But anyway, your mother can teach you how to cook on the show." Sera frowned. "In fact, why hasn't she?"

"When the equivalent of Julia Child is at home, why would she let anyone else mess around in the kitchen?" He shrugged. "Besides, I was always at hockey practice. I only made my own breakfast when I slept in. Everyone was doing what they did best. Mom in the kitchen, me on ice."

She smiled too sweetly. "You remember that scene in one of the *Star Wars* movies where Han Solo undergoes carbon-freezing...?"

"I know you'd love to put me on ice—" his expression turned seductive "—but you've heated me up instead."

"Jordan—"

"I like my name on your lips almost as much as your hair down." Instead of her usual ponytail, her hair was swinging loose for a change. Somehow, even with the scrubs she was wearing, the style made her look seductive. He fought the urge to touch her.

As if on cue, she held up a staying hand, and he schooled his expression.

"Right. Behave."

"As if you can."

"I'm trying. And your appearance on my mother's cooking show would help hold me to the bargain."

She sighed in exasperation. "Let's get started on your exercises for today."

He flashed a grin. "So that's a yes? You'll do it?"

"It depends."

"On what?"

"Your behavior. Fortunately, we're already in phase two of your rehabilitation."

"Great, so you're rehabilitating my knee and my playboy ways at the same time. Impressive."

She arched her brows. "I didn't say yes, but just call me a multitasker anyway. Today we'll be focusing on improving your strength base and balance."

As it turned out, the exercises she introduced him to in the gym were some he was familiar with from his pre-injury workouts. He had no trouble with leg squats and glut extensions, and then the various resistance exercises that she threw at him. All the while, Sera evaluated and corrected his body alignment and positioning.

Jordan concentrated on keeping his mind on the exercises. Focus was something that he normally excelled at, but with Sera nearby, he found that his concentration was shot. Instead, his mind wandered to the fullness of her lips, the softness of her skin and the pleasure of her occasional touch.

"We're looking for symmetry of right and left in your gait," she told him.

And he was looking for a *yes* to his proposition, so he aimed to please. At the end of their session, he couldn't resist asking, "So how did I do?"

"Great."

He winked. "And my reward is…?"

"I'll speak to the agent who handles my public appearances and get back to you."

He just laughed—because he was willing to chalk up anything other than an outright *no* as a win.

Eight

Sometimes it was good to catch up with teammates. Marc Bellitti and Vince Tedeschi lived just outside Springfield, where the Razors were based, so even in the off-season, they were good for an occasional beer at the Puck & Shoot, or for lunch like they were having today at another of their customary haunts, Mac-Dougal's Steakhouse.

Except today, Jordan had a motive for asking them to meet up. "I need your help."

With a cooking show. He'd debated how to float the idea of making an appearance on her program to his mother. He knew she'd be delighted to have one of her children back on the air. And Jordan's star power in particular couldn't hurt—just as when his new sister-in-law, Chiara Feran, the Hollywood actress, had gone on

the show. Debating what tactic he'd take since talking
to Sera and finally getting a tentative commitment, he'd
hit upon the idea of a cooking competition—among
hometown-team hockey players. Sort of like *Iron Chef*
with an ice-puck spin, and Sera as the judge. *Brilliant.*
His mother had loved it.

All he needed was to recruit a couple of his
teammates—and c'mon, they had to have time to
burn in the off-season, and a little positive publicity
couldn't hurt.

"When don't you need our help?" Marc joked, snag-
ging a remaining fry from their burger lunch. "Need
advice on how to talk to women? I'm your man."

If there was anyone who could best him in the
smart-aleck department, it was Marc. But Jordan held
his fire, because—as much as this pained him—he
needed Marc to play along here. And not in the way
his teammate probably imagined. Aloud, he said, "It
involves Vince, too."

From across the table, the Razors' goalie held up
his hands. "I'm good. Whatever scheme you two are
coming up with, count me out."

"Vince, if it's about women, believe me, you could
use all the help you can get," Marc shot back.

On that score, Jordan had to agree. Vince Tedeschi
was a big, hulking, taciturn guy. He was the team's
rock, but he let others do the razzle-dazzle.

"It's 'cause you're such a straight arrow that you're
perfect for this gig, Vince," Jordan said.

"Which is?" the goalie asked warily.

"I need you and Marc to cook." Jordan paused. "On
air. On my mother's show."

Vince groaned.

"Hey, you're used to being on television."

"But not cooking, man."

"It'll impress the ladies. They'll be calling and writing in."

Vince knitted his brow. "What's the demographic of *Flavors of Italy with Camilla Serenghetti*? My grandmother watches."

Next to Vince, Marc swallowed a snort. "And there's your answer right there."

"You won't be the only ones on it."

Now Marc looked intrigued.

"My physical therapist will be judging our cook-off."

Now Marc burst out laughing. "Great, I'll have a chance to kick your butt on air."

"Yeah, think of it as a golden opportunity," Jordan said drily.

Marc liked to indulge in the occasional prank, and Jordan had had his butt slapped by a hockey stick on more than one occasion.

"You've recruited your physical therapist, too?" Vince seemed perplexed.

"Serafina Perini," Jordan said. "She's an in-law."

Marc's brows shot up. "Do tell."

Jordan shrugged. "She's Cole's wife's cousin."

Vince grumbled. "Jeez."

Marc raised his hand. "Hold up, Tedeschi. Is this Serafina under eighty?"

"Yup." Jordan was tight-lipped.

"Single."

"Yeah." Jordan didn't like the direction this conversation was heading.

"Attractive?"

Jordan narrowed his eyes.

Marc rubbed his chin again. "Sounds like a woman to get to know."

And Jordan was feeling the urge to rearrange Marc's pretty face. He hadn't been able to get Sera out of his mind ever since their night together. Being around her was like a euphoric high that he'd only experienced one other place—on the ice. He was restless to see her, touch her, spar with her again.

"Wait, wait." Marc rubbed his chin. "Serafina Perini is ringing a bell… Was she the gorgeous ash-blonde poured into a satin dress at Cole and Marisa's surprise wedding?"

The way Jordan saw it, Marc's great memory could be a pain in the ass sometimes. He made a mental note not to invite the Razors' defenseman to any other weddings—not that he was planning to host one himself. "Her hair is a honey blond."

"You noticed." Marc flashed a knowing and triumphant grin.

"Just setting the record straight."

"Hey, is this the same Serafina who recently waitressed at the Puck & Shoot?" Vince suddenly piped up. "That woman you were chatting up during our last time there addressed the waitress as Serafina, and that's kind of an unusual name."

Jordan bit back a grimace—now Vince had to get all verbose on him? "I was not chatting up Danica. She walked over to me, and I was being polite."

"*Polite* is not the adjective that comes to mind, Serenghetti," Marc joked.

Jordan sat back and draped his arm along the top of their booth. "Hilarious."

"Serafina didn't seem particularly friendly toward you at the Puck & Shoot," Vince observed.

Jordan regarded both his teammates. Since when had the Razors' goalie become an astute observer of human interactions? "So are you guys going to do the show?"

Marc looked like he was enjoying himself and not ready to give up the fun. "So this Serafina is an in-law, your physical therapist, a waitress at the Puck & Shoot who, come to think of it, I should have recognized from your brother's wedding even if she was dressed up...and the special guest on your mother's show?" he drawled, rubbing his chin. "Seems as entangled as you've ever been with a woman, Serenghetti."

Jordan shrugged and adopted a bored tone. "Sera cooks, and Mom's liked her since her cousin married Cole."

Marc looked at Vince like he wanted to crack up. "Well, if your mother likes her, I guess that seals the deal."

"Not quite," Jordan replied drily. "I've got to get you two jokers to add some suspense to the whole episode."

"Not romance?" The defenseman adopted an exaggerated expression of shock.

"It's a cooking competition, Bellitti."

"And has this honey-blond physical therapist ever wanted to be on air?" Marc joked.

"No. And she's not into hockey guys." It couldn't hurt to drive the point home.

Marc's eyes crinkled. "Meaning you've failed with her? The legendary Jordan Serenghetti charm hasn't worked."

"I haven't tried." He hadn't tried to get to bed with her. Not really. Not yet...

"This I might have to see," Marc said, warming to the subject.

"If you go on the show, I'll prove that I can make Sera melt." A little extra motivation would be good for Marc.

The defenseman laughed again.

"Guys..." Vince said warningly.

"You're on, Serenghetti," Marc said, his eyes gleaming. "I'll let my agent know. Because I think you're not going to win."

"Don't be too sure."

"And when you do lose," Marc persisted, "what do I get?"

"The satisfaction of knowing I failed."

The Razors' defenseman laughed again. "I'm magnanimous. I'll hold to my side of the bargain, even if you haven't accomplished yours by the time the show tapes."

"Merciful is your middle name, Bellitti," Jordan remarked drily.

Vince shifted in his seat and muttered, "I've got a bad gut about this..."

"We know, Vince. You're out of this bet," Jordan said resignedly. "As far as you're concerned, you've seen no evil, heard no evil. Just do me a favor? Show up and do the program. And if you can outcook Bellitti, it'll be a bonus."

* * *

Sera couldn't believe she'd agreed to this. But here she was, in Camilla's office, eyeing Jordan and waiting to tape a cooking show. They'd already gone through the necessary paperwork with producers, and they'd met with Jordan's mother. Camilla Serenghetti was her usual bundle of energy.

Tipped off by Jordan, Sera had dressed in what she considered appropriate: a solid blue sweater and slacks—soon to be covered by an apron, anyway. Jordan had mentioned, and she'd known herself, that busy patterns didn't work on camera. She'd donned some delicate jewelry and had done her own hair and makeup—though she figured the show's staff would do some touch-up before she went on air.

They were in a lull while Camilla spoke with her producers on set and they waited for other guests and the audience to arrive and taping to begin. After she'd reluctantly committed to doing the show—thinking of Dante, Camilla and the favor she owed Jordan after her car accident—Jordan had informed her that the taping would be a cooking competition with him and a couple of Razors teammates as contestants *and her as the judge.* It had been too late to back out, but she couldn't help feeling a little bit like the star of *The Bachelorette*, being asked to choose among several single men.

Still, she felt poised, professional…and sexy under Jordan's regard. She had to put that night behind her— even though every time she was near him now, she had to fight the urge to touch him, slip back into his arms, and… *No, no, no.* Still, his magnetism was so strong, she could feel the pull as if it were a tangible force.

Ignoring the frisson of awareness that coursed through her at the thought, she focused on a framed photo of Jordan and his brothers when they were younger that rested on a nearby windowsill. Picking it up, she asked, "Is this you around age ten?"

Jordan tossed her a surprisingly sheepish smile. "No, that was me at twelve. I've hidden that photo every time I've been to Mom's office, but she keeps setting it back out." After a pause, he added, "I was a late bloomer."

Sensing a chance to rib him, Sera felt her lips twitch in a smile. "In other words, for the longest time, you were an underdeveloped, small and scrawny kid?"

"Going for the jugular with three adjectives, Perini? How about we leave it at *small*?"

"Wow, so you came late to your lady-killer ways..."

He bared his teeth. "How are they working?"

She resisted reminding him that he'd agreed to be on his best behavior today—her sanity depended on it. And she was still processing this new bit of information about Jordan. She'd assumed...well, she didn't know what she'd thought, but she'd always figured he'd sprung from the womb as a natural-born charmer. Apparently, she'd been—and, wow, it hurt to admit this—*wrong*.

"Braces on your teeth?" she asked, setting the photo back down.

"Check."

"Glasses?"

"Sometimes, until laser-vision surgery."

"Acne?"

He nodded. "I'll cop to the occasional teenage blemish."

"Nose job?"

"Now we're going too far."

She smirked. Rumor was, back in the day, all the Welsdale girls got boob jobs and cars for their birthdays—because they could.

"I leave the cosmetic surgery to the models and Hollywood starlets," he added, as if reading her mind.

At the reminder of the types of women he'd dated, she folded her arms. Because now they were back on comfortable ground. He'd started late, but he'd made up ground in the playboy arena with a vengeance. "Making up for lost time these days?"

"Let's not get all pop psychology on me."

No way was she backing off. She was enjoying this. Nodding at the picture, she asked, "How many of your dates have seen this?"

"None, fortunately. Not one has been in Mom's office. But *WE* Magazine ran a Before They Were Famous feature not long ago, and they dug up an old Welsdale newspaper article of me posing with my team in a youth-league photo."

"Horrors," she teased.

Jordan shrugged easily. "I got over it. Not even a nick in the public image."

"The carefully constructed persona stayed in place?"

"Fortunately for my sponsorship deals. Image is everything."

Sera widened her eyes. "Wow, so I just put it all together…"

"What?"

"Doctors, nurses, therapists. They're all uppermost in your subconscious."

"Hold on, Dr. Freud."

"You have a fixation with those in the health-care field because of your own sickly childhood."

Jordan arched a brow. "So you're saying that the reason I'm attracted to you is because you're a physical therapist?"

"Bingo," she concluded triumphantly, feeling a tingle of awareness at his admission that he wanted *her*.

"How much psychology have you studied?"

"I took a few courses on the way to my PT degree, but that's irrelevant."

"Right," he responded drily. "Here's another theory for you. I like blondes. See? My theory even has the beauty of simplicity."

Sera dropped her arms. "You're not taking me seriously."

Jordan tilted his head. "Don't you want to argue that my attraction to blondes stems from the newborn period? You know, when I might have been placed next to babies with wisps of light hair in the hospital?"

Sera resisted rolling her eyes.

"Hey, you started this. Anyway, does it matter? You're here, about to go on television—"

"Don't remind me."

"—and whether I like your physical-therapist scrubs or just women with cute blond ponytails is beside the point."

Sera reluctantly admitted he had a point. Still, if she could pigeonhole and rationalize their—uh, *his*—attraction, it would be easier to manage. Aloud, she said, "Why do you like me? You shouldn't, you know. We're bad for each other. I come with strings attached as an in-law, and that's contrary to your MO. And you're the type of on-and-off the field player that I think should come with a warning label."

"Maybe it's the forbidden aspect that drives the attraction."

"Maybe for you." *Damn it, he was right.*

"Okay, for me," he readily agreed and then checked his watch. "Ah, I've got to warn you before you go on—"

"What?" Sera's sublimated nervousness kicked up a notch.

"My father will be in the audience, and he has delusions of getting on television."

"He doesn't know your mother's show may get canceled?"

Jordan shook his head. "After his one guest appearance, he thinks he can make it better by becoming a staple on the program."

"And why not?" Sera asked. "He's about the only Serenghetti who hasn't been on television regularly."

Cole and Jordan had both been on televised NHL games, not to mention postgame interviews. Their brother, Rick, was a stuntman with movie credits who was married to a famous actress. Jordan's younger sister had done fashion shows that had been broadcast. And Camilla had her own television program, of course. Sera could understand why Serg felt left out of the limelight. He wasn't only dealing with his post-stroke infirmities but also with not appearing on the marquee alongside the rest of his family. As a physical therapist, she'd seen his frustration in plenty of patients and could sympathize.

"If he wants to be on television, he should consider commercials for a construction industry supplier instead," Jordan muttered.

"Then why hasn't he?"

"Because he fancies himself a sommelier these days."

Sera felt a tinkling laugh bubble up. "A wine expert?"

"Bingo. And guess whose show he thinks would be perfect for a regular guest segment."

"Oh."

"Right."

"Your father just wants to be understood."

Jordan snorted. "He's tough as nails and ornery."

Sera tilted her head. "So you're telling me this because he might spring up from his seat in the audience and shout something?"

"He can't spring up from anywhere these days," Jordan muttered. "And believe me, the only reason he'd shout a comment is to tell me I'm doing something wrong."

"Does he do that at your hockey games, too?" Sera asked, amused.

"If he does, he's too tucked away in the stands for people to really notice. Anyway, my point is he may try to insert himself into the show somehow, and I don't want you to be surprised by anything…unexpected."

"How does your mother feel about this turn of events?"

"Like the breadwinner who has a temperamental kid on her hands."

Sera laughed.

"Suddenly she's the star, and he's cast in her shadow. Though, I don't think he'd even admit to himself that's what he's feeling."

Sera tapped a finger against her lips. "There's got to be a solution to this."

Jordan shrugged. "If there is one, I haven't thought of it."

Just then, one of Camilla's producers stepped into the room to call them on set.

"Ready?" Jordan asked, searching her gaze.

Sera shrugged. "As ready as I'll ever be."

Showtime. In more ways than one...

Nine

She was supposed to have had one rule: never get involved with a player.

Except Jordan actually seemed kind of cute and endearing at the moment wearing an apron, but still looking masculine. He was prepared to make a fool of himself under the bright television-studio lights. All for the sake of his mother. *Aww.*

Sera straightened her spine against the traitorous thought. She needed to get him in top shape and marketable for Dante and his team—and his sponsors. *Nothing more.*

"Hi, Sera!" Marisa waved as she stepped into the studio with her husband and scanned for an empty seat.

Sera's eyes widened. "What are you doing here?"

"Returning the favor," Cole replied, shooting a look at Jordan.

"What favor?" Sera knew she sounded like a parrot, but she couldn't help herself.

She'd avoided mentioning her appearance on the show today to Marisa, which meant… She focused her gaze on Jordan, who wore a bland mask.

Cole cast his brother a sardonic look. "Jordan came as comic relief when Marisa and I were guests on Mom's cooking show before we were married."

"Oh." Sera remembered teasing her cousin about the significance of that appearance for her relationship with Cole—which was why she hadn't wanted to mention her own cameo today in return to Marisa, who might get the wrong idea.

"We thought about bringing Dahlia," her cousin went on, oblivious to Sera's distress, "but we figured she was too young to—"

"—watch her uncle Jordan get outmaneuvered." Cole chuckled.

"Thanks for the vote of confidence," Jordan replied.

Cole flashed a smile. "Payback, little brother."

"And thanks to the fact that Mom still has a show, you have the chance," Jordan grumbled.

Just then, Serg Serenghetti walked into the studio, all the while chatting with a producer.

"Excuse me," Cole said. "I'm going to help Dad find a seat."

Jordan watched his brother walk away and shrugged. "The Serenghettis have arrived in force."

Sera bit back a groan. *Great.*

As if on cue, more Serenghetti family members en-

tered the studio. Rick and Chiara Serenghetti were followed by Jordan's sister, Mia. Even though Chiara wore
glasses and a baseball cap, so as not to be identified as a
well-known actress, Sera recognized her immediately.

Sera swung back to Jordan and asked accusingly,
"What is this? A Serenghetti family reunion?"

Jordan shrugged. "News to me, too." Then he
stepped forward and addressed his middle brother.
"What are you doing here?"

"We're here for moral support," Rick replied sar-
donically.

"For whom?" Jordan replied.

Sera was wondering the same thing. In this wilder-
than-dreams scenario, it was hard to tell who needed
help more: her, Jordan or Camilla, whose show might
be in the crosshairs of new management.

Mia Serenghetti walked up, holding a cup of coffee
and looking on trend in the way only a budding fashion designer could. She caught Sera's gaze. "Nice job
bringing my youngest brother to heel."

Sera blew a breath. Despite her best intentions, it
was as if she and Jordan wore bright neon signs: *Get
These Two Together.* Still, as everyone laughed, Sera
pasted a smile on her face. "Thanks, Mia, but I'm not
in the market for—"

"—reforming bad boys," Jordan finished for her
wryly. "Yes, we know."

Mia's gaze swung from Sera to her youngest brother
and back. "Finishing each other's sentences. Interesting."

That comment earned a laugh from Rick and Chiara.

Sera held up her hands. "No, we're not. We're boring. Very, very boring."

"Better hope that's not true for the sake of Mom's show!" Mia replied, taking a sip of her coffee.

Fortunately, Sera was saved from the need for further comment because the studio staff—including the middle-aged producer who'd summoned her from Camilla's office earlier—started hustling everyone into position.

Minutes later, Sera pasted a smile on her face for the cameras and went with the agreed-upon script. "Gentlemen, start your kitchen appliances."

The audience chuckled.

Okay, so she was here as an *alleged* cooking expert to judge Jordan's kitchen skills against those of two Razors teammates he'd cajoled, charmed or blackmailed into appearing as contestants today.

Jordan was so in trouble. And frankly, so was she. When she'd agreed to this, she'd thought she was volunteering for some sedate affair. She should have known better with the Serenghettis.

"Jordan, let's start with you," Camilla said in a drill-sergeant tone as she stopped at his counter station.

"Playing favorites, Mom?" Jordan asked, and then winked at the camera. "I always knew I was first."

Camilla ignored him. "What will you be making?"

"*Pasta alla chitarra* with fresh mackerel ragù, capers, tomatoes and Taggiasca olives."

Sera couldn't help a look of surprise. She was shocked Jordan even knew what a Taggiasca olive was.

Jordan winked at the audience. "You can call this dish The Jordan Serenghetti Pasta Special."

Sera raised an eyebrow because Jordan seemed not the least bit nervous about his ambitious recipe. *Fine, let him try.* Shouldn't she have known by now that he was always up for a challenge?

Marc Bellitti volunteered that he'd be making a ravioli dish with a secret family recipe for vodka sauce. And Vince Tedeschi said he'd prepare *pollo alla cacciatore* with mussels.

"Thank you, Vinny." Sera tossed the Razors' goalie an encouraging smile because he seemed the most nervous of the contestants.

Jordan's brows drew into a straight line. "That's Vince."

"She can call me whatever she wants," Jordan's teammate responded with an easy grin.

Sera tossed him a beatific smile. "I'm a fan of turf and surf."

"It's *surf and turf,* not *turf and surf,*" Jordan said.

Sera ignored him. "Apparently, the only one who is allowed to make up names is Jordan himself."

"Oh, yeah?" Marc asked interestedly. "What does he call you?"

Sera and Jordan stared at each other for a moment, their gazes clashing.

The entire studio audience—including, heaven help her, Marisa, Cole *and* Camilla Serenghetti—seemed to lean in for the answer.

"Angel," she and Jordan said in unison to much laughter.

"Hey, I think this contest is rigged," Vince protested.

"Yes, but not in the way you think," Sera cooed. "I don't like the name."

"Great, we've neutralized the famous Serenghetti charm," Marc put in.

"We'll see," Jordan remarked drily.

Camilla Serenghetti hurried forward. "Let's get down to cooking."

"Before this show degenerates into slapstick comedy," Sera added.

When Vince groaned, Jordan arched a brow. "Don't you mean *hockey stick*?"

"There's no puck," Sera replied crisply. "We're slapping the joke into the goal for the winning shot."

"Hmm. The only thing you should be slapping is the fish for the entrée you're making."

The show proceeded smoothly after that. And Sera had to give Jordan points for trying. But at the end, after sampling all three dishes, she had to go with Vince's *pollo alla cacciatore* because it was simply superb. For the audience's benefit, she explained, "While I chose Vince's recipe, Marc Bellitti also gets points for a professional-quality family sauce. And Jordan's dish is original. They were all close…"

"I've always said Marc has the secret sauce," Vince joked. "On and off the ice."

"Hey, I thought that was me," Jordan chimed in.

Camilla clapped her hands. "Well, we have a winner—" she fixed her gaze on her son "—and a loser."

"So Jordan is hopeless?" Vince asked jokingly.

Camilla clasped her hands together. "Perhaps Sera would like to give my son a cooking lesson?"

Sera's eyes widened. No way was she signing up for more. "Signora Serenghetti, I—"

Camilla's request was a tall order. And she'd already told Jordan she wasn't into reforming bad boys. But they were on TV with a live audience—and Jordan was contemplating her expectantly. Looking around for a lifeline, her gaze came to rest on Serg Serenghetti in the audience, and an idea struck. "Serg, would you like to come up here and suggest a wine that I could pair with Vince's winning dish?"

She tossed a significant glance at Jordan and Camilla. "After all, if the loser might get a cooking lesson, the winner should receive some recognition, too."

Serg's face brightened.

"Well, *pollo alla cacciatore* is an interesting dish," Serg said, though he was already slowly standing. "It's got many blended flavors that you don't want to overwhelm. You still want to taste the tomatoes and mushrooms."

Cole got up to help him, but the older man batted away his hand.

"Oh, come on, Signor Serenghetti, I'm sure you can suggest something," Sera prompted.

Serg chuckled. "Well, sure, if you insist."

"Oh, I do." Sera was enjoying herself. Beside her, Camilla and Jordan had gone still. *Priceless.* She bit back a laugh as Serg stole everyone's thunder. Jordan was probably wondering whether she'd gone nuts and why she was disregarding his warning from earlier. But she had a plan.

Serg accepted help from a producer who gave him a hand getting on stage and led him to where Sera was standing. "Now, traditional chicken *cacciatore* is made with red wine—"

Sera furrowed her brow at the camera for effect.

"—but Vince went with white instead."

Sera widened her eyes to underscore the point.

"Obviously, he would not have won if the dish wasn't creative and delicious," Serg added.

"Of course."

"Now a Chianti classico is a good red wine to pair with traditional *pollo alla cacciatore*." Serg paused. "But even a white zinfandel would be good paired with Vince's version."

"A Serenghetti who knows his wine," Sera offered approvingly.

"My son—" Serg jerked his thumb at Jordan "—never offered you a glass of wine?"

Sera heated, and Jordan cleared his throat.

"Well, uh—"

"As a matter of fact—"

The older Serenghetti cut them both off. "A travesty."

"We've had catering at family events. I've never had to bartend," Jordan offered by way of explanation to the audience.

"And I like to pour my own wine," Serafina added quickly, trying to cut off the line of conversation, which could end up…who knew where.

Serg just shook his head in disappointment.

Steering the conversation to safer ground, Sera said, "You're a natural at this."

Serg beamed, while Jordan tossed her a questioning look that said *You're creating a monster.*

Ignoring Jordan's expression, Sera went on. "You should have your own gig, Mr. Serenghetti, not minutes snatched from another show. You could tape commercial-length wine segments." She smiled brightly. "I've even got a name. *Wine Breaks with Serg!*"

The audience clapped in approval.

Before Serg could respond, a producer signaled Camilla, who stepped forward.

"Alla prossima volta," Camilla said, giving her signature closing line. "Till next time, *buon appetito.*"

Seconds later, the cameras switched off, and Sera's gaze tangled with Jordan's.

He gave a relieved and appreciative grin. "Nice moves. Thanks for giving Dad his cameo and for suggesting something else for him to do. I wouldn't be surprised if he went straight home to build his business plan."

"No trouble," Sera mumbled before looking away in confusion. She had the warm fuzzies from his compliment, and she so didn't want that feeling where Jordan was concerned. Even mindless sexual attraction to a marquee brand, a celebrity face and a bad-boy body was preferable. Because emotion meant wading into dangerous, deeper waters.

"If Dad has his own project, it'll take the heat off Mom." Jordan shrugged. "And who knows? In the future, she might feel comfortable enough to partner with him on air, once he's got his own audience. Good going."

Sera blew some wisps of hair away from her face.

Why hadn't she noticed how hot it was under the studio lights when they'd been taping? "I like my entertainment with unexpected plot twists."

Jordan laughed. "What a coincidence. So do I."

His siblings came up on stage then, and Jordan turned away to deal with his family.

Sera found herself at momentary loose ends, until her cousin Marisa stepped close, a teasing expression on her face. "You know you're in trouble, right?"

"I was hoping the trouble was over."

Her cousin shook her head. "Nope. Every woman who has been on this show to cook alongside a Serenghetti has wound up married to him."

Sera felt her stomach somersault, but she strove not to show emotion. "Don't worry. There's no chance of that in this case."

She'd sworn Jordan to secrecy, and in any case, their one recent encounter was eons away from a march down the aisle. Marisa angled her head, scanning her expression. "Are you sure there's nothing more between you and Jordan?"

Sera scoffed. "Of course. Positive."

"Well, I'll just repeat what you said to me," Marisa said, and she mimicked Sera's voice. "'He wants you to appear on his mother's cooking show? That's serious.'"

"That's some memory you have," Sera grumbled.

Her cousin just smiled.

Sera bit back a groan. *Out of the frying pan and into the fire.*

Sera hurried out the front doors of St. Vincent's Hospital to greet the sunny afternoon outside. She'd just visited one of her patients who'd had to have additional surgery.

She was back to business as usual—or so she told herself—after taping Camilla's show two days ago. She hadn't heard from Jordan but she was scheduled to see him again soon for their weekly therapy session. Anticipation shivered over her skin.

She'd known her family would eventually see or hear about her appearance on Camilla's show, so she'd played it off as doing a favor for Jordan and the rest of the Serenghettis. Dante had been thrilled.

Head bowed, she dropped her cell phone into her handbag as she blinked against the bright sunshine, and then collided with a rock-solid chest. "Oomph!"

Strong hands grasped her arms and steadied her. "Easy."

She looked up and locked gazes with the last person she expected to see right now. *Jordan.*

"I didn't think I'd run into you here," he said, dropping his arms and stepping aside.

She followed suit so she wasn't standing in the way of pedestrian traffic. "I just finished visiting an elderly patient of mine who needed surgery." Sera searched her brain for pleasantries even as she drank him in— he looked sinfully good. "What are you doing here?"

"I work with the Once upon a Dream Foundation. I'm visiting the pediatric floor."

She couldn't keep the surprised look from her face.

"Want to join me?" Jordan asked.

Sera looked around and noticed he was alone.

Jordan's eyes crinkled. "I don't normally bring a camera crew with me on these visits." He shrugged.

"I prefer not to make it a media event. Sometimes the kids like it when they're on the news, but other times it freaks them out."

"I'd think a kid would freak out just because Jordan Serenghetti showed up in his hospital room."

Jordan grinned and nodded toward the entrance. "Then, come inside with me and calm things down. You're good at puncturing my ego."

Sera flushed. "Yup, you're right."

He was easy on the eyes and, now that she didn't have quite as many of her negative conceptions of him, *dangerous*. Today was another blow to her armor—he did charity work with sick kids?

"So what do you say, Angel? Ready to head back in?"

She couldn't even get annoyed about his use of the pet name at the moment. She was a sucker for people in need—and those who helped them. It was why she'd become a physical therapist. "Another appearance with you in front of a live audience? How could I refuse?"

Jordan gave her a lopsided grin. "Before long, you'll be a pro."

That was what she was afraid of. Nevertheless, she turned to follow him into the main hospital building. He placed a guiding hand at the small of her back, and she felt his touch radiate out from her center, heating her.

Upstairs, the nurses broke into smiles when Jordan appeared. As brief greetings were exchanged, Sera wondered how many other sick kids Jordan had visited in the past.

A portly middle-aged woman in scrubs pulled a hockey stick out of a closet next to the nurse's station.

"Thanks, Elsie," Jordan said, flashing a killer smile as he took the equipment from her.

"Anything for you, honey," Elsie teased. "My husband knows I'm a fan."

Catching Sera's expression, Jordan looked sheepish. "I came by yesterday, but it was the wrong moment for a visit. Elsie was kind enough to hold on to the hockey stick until I came back."

Moments later, another nurse directed them down the hall. When they stopped at an open patient-room door, Sera waited for Jordan to enter first.

He rapped on the door and then stepped inside. Immediately, there was whooping and hollering from a handful of adults in addition to a boy who was sitting up in his hospital bed.

Sera paused on the threshold. Of course she knew Jordan had a fan base, but seeing his effect on people in person was another thing. At the Puck & Shoot, he was surrounded by regulars who weren't surprised when he showed up. And Sera had always dismissed a lot of the rest as just the adulation of adoring, unthinking women. But now, when she saw the frail and bald boy sitting up in his bed—he couldn't be more than ten or twelve—and how his eyes lit up at the sight of Jordan, emotion welled up inside her.

Stepping over the threshold, Sera scanned the crowd. An assortment of adults continued to laugh and smile.

"Hey, Brian. What's going on?" Jordan said casually.

Brian broke into a grin. "Number Twenty-six. I can't believe you're here."

Sera recognized the number as the one that Jordan wore. The local shops in Welsdale sold that jersey more than any other.

"Hey, you invited me," Jordan joked. "Of course I'd show up."

"Yeah, but you're busy."

"Not too busy to visit one of my best fans."

Brian looked uncertain. "I am?"

"You used your wish on me."

A grin appeared again. "Yeah, I did. I just can't believe it worked."

Brian's assorted visitors laughed—including two who, from the resemblance, could be Brian's parents.

Sera felt her smile become tremulous. Damn Jordan Serenghetti. He made her mad, sad and bad by turns—she was always riding a roller coaster in his company.

As the adults talked, Sera learned that Brian's prognosis was good. His leukemia was responding to treatment.

"I brought you something," Jordan said to Brian.

"The hockey stick is for me?"

"Of course. What would a visit be without memorabilia? And I'm going to sign it, too." Jordan fished a marker out of his pocket and placed his signature on the widest part. Then he handed the stick to Brian.

"Wow! Thanks."

"I hope you enjoy it."

Brian looked up from his gift. "Do you think you'll be playing again soon?"

"I hope so." Then Jordan turned to nod in the direction of the doorway. "Sera's the one who's making sure I'll be back on the ice."

"She's your doctor?"

Sera flushed. Such an innocent question, and such a complicated answer. *Hired professional, in-law and…*

Jordan chuckled. "She's medical. Definitely one of the scrubs."

She cleared her throat as everyone's gaze swung to her. "I'm his physical therapist. We, um, crossed paths downstairs after I saw another patient, and Jordan was kind enough to invite me along on this visit. I hope you don't mind."

Her voice trailed off as she finished her lame and rambling explanation. *Not a girlfriend, not a girlfriend, not a girlfriend.* Thank goodness there were no television cameras in the room.

"Hey, Brian, let's get some pictures of you with Jordan," someone piped up after a moment.

Sera was glad for the change of topic.

Obligingly, Jordan stepped forward and leaned in so that someone could snap a photo. Afterward, Jordan lingered for another quarter of an hour, talking with Brian and the others.

Sera chatted with a woman who introduced herself as Brian's mother and also with a nurse who stopped in. A half hour later, as Brian yawned a couple of times, Jordan took his cue, and Sera followed his lead in saying goodbye.

As she and Jordan made their way toward the elevator bank, she remarked, "You were the highlight of his day."

Jordan sighed, suddenly serious. "It's tough sometimes. Not all of the kids get better, but their courage is inspiring."

"You lift their spirits."

His lips quirked. "It's the least I can do if I'm not going to heal their bodies with physical therapy."

Sera flushed as she stepped into an empty elevator, and he followed. "Do you volunteer here because you were a sick kid yourself?"

"Going all pop psychology on me again, Angel?"

"Just an observation based on the evidence," she remarked as the doors closed.

"Okay, yeah."

"So I was wrong," she joked. "You don't have a fetish for Florence Nightingale types."

Jordan quirked an eyebrow. "I don't? What a relief."

Sera shook her head as the elevator opened again on the ground-floor lobby. "No, my new theory is that you want to be Florence."

Jordan stifled a laugh as they crossed the lobby to the exit. "Great. I guess I have my costume for next Halloween."

When they emerged from the building, she turned to face him. "Would you be serious?"

"Would you?"

"Your visit today was a nice thing to do."

He flashed a boyish grin. "See, I'm not all bad."

"No, no, you're not."

"So I'm making progress?"

"Of sorts."

"Good enough."

"I can't fault a guy who visits sick kids." She cleared her throat. "I had an older sister who died as a baby."

Jordan sobered.

She adjusted her handbag. "She died from a congenital defect." She wasn't sure why she was volunteering the information. "Your family may have hovered because you were always sick. Mine did, too, but for different reasons."

"They were protective because they knew what it meant to lose a child," he guessed.

"Exactly, though it was hard for me to appreciate at the time." She didn't want to understand Jordan Serenghetti, but she did—more and more. It was much easier to label him as just another player.

"My sister Mia could tell you all about overprotective parents." Jordan gave Sera a half smile.

She thought back to her brief conversation with Jordan's sister on set the other day, then sighed as she remembered something else from the taping. "I hope your mother isn't still expecting me to teach you how to cook."

Jordan flashed her a teasing look. "Don't worry—"

"Phew! What a relief." So why did she feel disappointed suddenly?

"I've gotten you off the hook by telling her that I'd ask you to attend a wedding with me."

Sera's mind went blank. "Wait—what?"

"A wedding. I avoid them like the plague—"

"Of course you do."

"—but this one I have to attend. It's a cousin, and Mom is all about family."

Well, that might explain why all the Serenghettis were in town—Mia from New York, where she was based, and Rick and Chiara from Los Angeles. They were here for a wedding—as well as to throw moral support behind Camilla *and* bear witness to Sera's onscreen chemistry with the family's baddest bad boy.

"That is some stealthy maneuvering, Serenghetti," Sera said in her sternest voice.

"It was Mom's idea."

"What!"

"She suggested I bring you to the wedding instead." Jordan shrugged too casually. "Because I was planning to fly solo."

"She makes a good accomplice," Sera muttered.

Jordan gave a short laugh. "She's desperate."

"For ratings, or to get you paired up with a woman who likes to use her brain?"

"Maybe both." Jordan schooled his expression. "You have to come with me to the wedding. I'm too injured to find a date."

"Please. You'd be able to find a date even from a hospital bed."

"You're giving me too much credit."

"Modesty. What a refreshing change for you," she teased. "So I'm a last resort?"

He looked like a kid caught with his hand in the cookie jar. "And a first."

She searched his expression, saw only earnestness and then felt warmth suffuse her.

She didn't want to be number one in Jordan's book—did she?

Ten

The last place Sera wanted to be was at an event with more Serenghettis—and yet here she was.

She'd been to enough get-togethers at Marisa and Cole's house or Serg and Camilla's to know the Serenghettis welcomed everyone and anyone. But once a social event ventured into cousin or—heaven help her—even second-cousin territory, like today's wedding, she knew she was in deep. In fact, she'd just met another of Jordan's second cousins, Gia Serenghetti, so now she knew the family's inside joke about the rhyming Mia and Gia "twins."

Still, Sera had to admit the colonial mansion outside Springfield, Massachusetts, was a picture-perfect setting for a June wedding. She'd decided to wear a sleeveless shimmering emerald sheath dress for the evening affair, and she'd caught back her hair in a jeweled clip for a low ponytail.

Jordan's gaze lit as it settled on her again from across the lawn, where he stood chatting with some fellow guests during the postceremony cocktail reception, while the bride and groom, Constance Marche and Oliver Serenghetti, posed for picturesque photos on the lawn. His perusal was a slow burn, full of promises and possibilities as it skimmed her curves.

As she took a sip of champagne, Sera could almost read the thoughts chasing through his mind. She was a flame dancing in the warm breeze of his appreciation. *Wow.*

Still, she felt like a phony. An impostor. She wasn't really Jordan's girlfriend or even his date. She was here as a fill-in, to avoid a cooking lesson that had been asked for on air. And to help Dante. And...*nothing more.*

She was so far from getting married herself, she might as well have been in a different galaxy. Neil had seen to that. And it wasn't as if she and Jordan would ever walk down the aisle. Her heart squeezed, nevertheless. She'd gotten misty-eyed at the exchange of vows earlier. It had been so beautiful, so perfect. The couple caught in the beams of the evening sun behind them and outlined by a trellis with climbing flowers. She couldn't think of a better arrangement if she'd been planning her own ceremony—not that it was in the cards.

On top of it, Marisa kept shooting her quizzical looks—as if her cousin, too, was puzzled about what to make of today and Sera's agreement to appear on Jor-

dan's arm, especially since Sera had sworn that there
was nothing romantic between her and Jordan. An appearance on Jordan's mother's show was one thing; a
family wedding was another. *That's serious.* Her cousin's words echoed in her head.

Jordan approached, and Sera noticed again how he
filled out his dark tailored suit. Only her well-trained
eye could detect any lingering unevenness in his gait,
since they were now more than two months postsurgery. In the past couple of weeks, since the cooking
show, he'd grown stronger and more able with each
physical-therapy session. Even she had been impressed
at his progress. She knew from experience that there
could be many unexpected stumbling blocks to recovery.

"I should never have agreed to this," Sera murmured
as Jordan stopped by her side.

He took a sip from his champagne. "Relax. It's not
as if we were caught having sex in the closet under
the hall stairs."

"There's a closet under the stairs?" she squeaked.
Why was she turned on? She wanted to fan herself
and instead took another fortifying sip from her glass.

Jordan gave a strangled laugh. "Every old mansion
has one."

"There's already open speculation in your family about what the status is between the two of us. I
can read the looks on their faces, and they don't even
know—"

"—we got it going already?"

Sera nodded, her face warming. "This is getting
complicated."

"No, it's simple. You don't like me, and I've got a hard case of lust for you."

"I've been rethinking that part," she muttered.

"What?"

She cast him a sidelong look. "The part about how I don't...don't like you."

Jordan fiddled with the knot of his tie. "Now you tell me?" he joked. "We're at a wedding surrounded by a couple of hundred people. Some of them even related to me."

"And whose fault is that?" she replied. "Isn't there a closet under the stairs where we can hide?"

Jordan gave her a look of such longing and heat that Sera felt as if her clothes evaporated right off her.

He leaned close and whispered in her ear. "Hiding isn't exactly what I had in mind."

"Oh?" she asked breathlessly.

"What's under that dress?"

"It's got a built-in bra," she answered hesitantly.

"Even better. One zipper? I want to know how easy it is to peel you out of it."

"It's on the back. But don't you want to explore and find the exits on your own?"

Jordan took a deep swallow of his drink. "We could do this."

This was so crazy. They were actually contemplating if they could duck inside the mansion for a quickie.

"Dinner will start soon," she tried.

"We won't be missed."

"Is that why you waited till now? Because disappearing from the ceremony would have been too noticeable?" She really needed a fan.

One side of his mouth rose in a slight smile. "You think you were saved by the wedding bell?"

"Maybe you've been." Jordan was a no-strings kind of guy—it would be lethal if he was caught getting it on with her, of all people, and here, of all places.

"Angel, it's not salvation…yet. It's purgatory right now."

Sera forced a laugh. "Hey, you invited me to this event. I'm sure all your relatives aside from your mother are surprised you're here with a date." *Me*.

"Let them wonder all they want. It's been way too long."

"Since you've been at a wedding?"

"Since the two of us have been all over each other with lust," he responded bluntly.

Sera sucked in a breath.

"Don't tell me you haven't been wondering, too," Jordan continued in a low, deep voice. "Fantasizing about whether the chemistry that night in my apartment was a fluke or we're really that good together."

In fact, she had. She'd been working hard to keep up her defenses, but it hadn't worked. She was having trouble remembering why she shouldn't like him. "Okay, I have. But it's unprofessional of me—"

Jordan gave a dismissive laugh.

"—and wrong." Dangerous, even. To her peace of mind.

He took the champagne flute from her hand and set it down on a nearby table along with his own glass. Then taking her hand, he said, "Come on."

She looked startled. "What? Where? Why?"

"You forgot *when* and *how*." He tossed her a wicked

glance as they headed toward the back of the mansion. "*When* is now, and the answer to *how* is that there's a cloakroom off the main hall on the ground floor that isn't being used because it's summer and no one brought a coat. It's also bigger than the closet under the stairs."

Sera's quick indrawn breath was audible. Still, excitement bubbled up within her. They were playing with fire, but she felt alive, all her senses awakened.

They slipped inside the house without drawing attention, and in line with Jordan's expectations, the short hallway to the cloakroom was deserted. He opened the half door and then led her toward the shadowed recesses.

The minute they reached the back wall, his mouth was on hers.

Finally. She exulted in being in his arms again. She'd fought the good fight against his charm, but everything except this moment receded into the background.

Their mixed sighs filled the empty room as the kiss deepened. She tunneled her fingers into his hair, and he pulled her closer. All her soft curves pressed into his hard, lean physique, molding to him.

His scent was so good, his taste even better. And her senses stirred with his kiss, which was hot, warm and enticing.

When the kiss finally broke off, Jordan skimmed his mouth across her cheek and nuzzled her temple before his breath settled around the delicate shell of her ear, giving her goosebumps and making her weak with awareness.

"Your dress has been driving me crazy all evening," he muttered.

"It's not meant to make men wild with lust."

He gave a strangled laugh. "That keyhole cutout that shows your cleavage. All I wanted to do was this—" he reached to her nape, and her zipper rasped downward "—and bare your gorgeous breasts."

She leaned against the wall, her breath hissing out of her as the top of her gown sagged. She wanted—

In the next moment, Jordan unerringly gave her what she was seeking—cupping her exposed breast and running his thumb over the pebbled peak.

"You're so responsive, Sera," he whispered, his voice reverent.

She shifted, brushing against his erection, and they both sighed.

Jordan bent and covered her breast with his mouth, and her hands tunneled through his hair as she gave herself up to waves of sensation that carried her closer to a shore of paradise...

Suddenly, there was the sound of a door opening, and Sera froze, yanked from a wonderful reverie.

Jordan straightened, and they hastily moved apart.

Sera's gaze met Jordan's in the shadows, and he pulled her closer, yanking the top of her dress back into place as he did so.

"Shh," he whispered into her ear.

Obediently, she stood still, hoping not to be noticed.

"I'll be back in New York on Monday," a woman's voice said. "We can discuss it then."

Jordan relaxed, his hold on her easing.

Sera thought it sounded like—

"Thanks, Sonia." There was a rustle, as if someone was fiddling with her purse.

In the next moment, the cloakroom was flooded with light as someone flipped a switch.

"Jordan."

Sera suppressed a groan. It was definitely Jordan's sister.

"Mia."

While Jordan stayed pressed against her for obvious reasons, Sera looked sideways over her shoulder at his sister, who wore an amused expression.

"I was just helping Sera with her dress." Jordan shrugged. "Stuck zipper."

"Of course," Mia played along. "You don't need to tell me. As a fashion designer, I've seen dozens. Hundreds, even. Those darn zippers. The pesky things give the worst trouble at the most inconvenient moments."

"Right," Jordan agreed.

"Sometimes a zipper will open easily but get stuck closing, or the reverse. Was the zipper going up or down?"

"For God's sake, Mia."

Sera's face flamed. Could things get more mortifying? And of course, it had to be one of Jordan's siblings who walked in on them.

"What are you doing here, Mia?" Jordan asked, going on the offensive.

"I could ask the same thing of you, big brother. But for the record, I was looking for a quiet place to take a call and just wandered in this direction right when the call was ending." Mia arched a brow. "And I'm going to assume you two came this way looking for a sewing kit…to fix Sera's dress."

Sera's hands flew to her cheeks.

Mia laughed. "Don't worry, your secret is safe with me." She gestured near her mouth as if turning a key in her lips and throwing it away.

"Thanks, sis."

Mia winked at them and then flipped the light switch and threw them into darkness again.

A moment later, Sera heard footsteps receding down the hall. She collapsed against Jordan with a small sound of relief, even though she wasn't sure how much longer she could stand their sexual frustration.

As Jordan drove her home after the wedding, Sera was a bundle of tingling awareness. They'd managed to keep their hands off each other and the PDAs to a minimum through the wedding dinner and dancing and socializing, but the tension had built…and built.

Yes, she'd been embarrassed about being caught in a clinch by Mia. And she hoped that Jordan's sister could keep a secret. But she and Jordan were playing with fire, and it just fueled their sizzling attraction.

They got out of his car and made their way to her building, enjoying the fresh air on this warm and balmy night. There was no question she was inviting him upstairs and inside. In the hall outside her front door, she handed him her keys, and the gesture—a mere brush of the fingers—was electric.

When Jordan pushed open the door, Sera entered the silent apartment and turned on a dim lamp. She hadn't changed much of Marisa's decor for the two-bedroom apartment, which had a retro vibe—right down to the Unblemished Yellow wall paint that her cousin had used to give a face-lift to the old kitchen cabinets. She was home, and yet her place had never felt less relaxed. Instead, the air was charged with sexual tension.

She heard every rustle as she set down her evening bag on a console table and Jordan followed her. With a remote, she switched on some flameless candles that sat on a chest in her living room and then turned and nearly collided with Jordan's chest.

He ducked his head and kissed her—all sexy and lingering.

Sera leaned into the kiss. She wanted to taste him, lick him, be enveloped by him.

When they broke apart, he gazed into her eyes. "I want you, Sera. I can't stop thinking about you."

And just like that, the shackles broke, and Sera was in his arms, kissing him back and pressing closer, desperate to pick up where they had left off earlier in the evening.

"Jordan," she breathed.

He smoothed his hands along her curves and skimmed kisses from her mouth to the side of her neck.

She'd resisted him for weeks but had nevertheless felt herself sliding into an attraction that she could not deny. He'd been hard to ignore—at physical therapy, on his mother's cooking show, in the hospital, and now at a wedding—and impossible to resist. He'd seduced her in the process, teasing her out of her shell.

He tugged on the zipper at the back of her dress and it rasped downward, her breasts spilling against him out of the built-in bra.

Bracing his good knee on a nearby ottoman, he bent and drew her closer. Running his hand up her calf in a light caress, he pulled one breast into his mouth.

She held his head close, her eyes falling shut. *Bliss.* The sensations were so acute, so exquisite, and she knew it all had to do with him and their burning, simmering desire for each other.

Jordan transferred his attention to her other breast, and Sera moaned.

He slid his hands up her legs, pushing up the hem of her dress, and then hooked his hands inside the band of her panties and pulled them down.

Sera braced her hands on his shoulders.

He murmured sweet encouragement and words of appreciation. "I've wanted you so long. Waited for you."

Me, too.

It was her last thought before he tugged her down to the ottoman, where she lay back, bracing herself on her elbows as he bent in front of her.

He ran his hands up and down her thighs in a delicious caress. Eventually, he found her with his mouth, and a strangled cry was torn from her lips. She lost all sense of time, just letting herself feel all the wicked things that he was doing to her. And then suddenly, her climax was upon her in a bright burst of energy.

She spasmed, riding an intense crest of pleasure that went on and on until she floated down and went limp against him.

Somehow, after that, they found their way to the bedroom, where they both stripped off the rest of their clothes.

She loved him with her mouth and hands until she could sense Jordan was on the brink of losing control.

"Ah, Sera," he groaned.

"Too much?" she teased as she settled back on her bed.

"Just right." He sheathed himself in protection and braced himself over her.

She quirked a brow at him. "Came prepared, did you?"

He flashed a quick grin. "Wishful thinking, but thank you. It's because of your therapy that we're even able to use this sexual position."

"Sure, blame me," she teased again.

He gave a strangled laugh. "No, I'm going to love you until we're both mindless."

In the next instant, he stroked inside her, and they both sighed.

She took up the tempo that he set. Sera had never felt so close to anyone before.

She'd rationalized away their first encounter on the night of the car accident as the product of adrenaline, annoyance and more.

But this time, there was no denying the truth. She came again, clinging to him as he sent her soaring on a wave of pleasure right before he found his own release.

In the aftermath, she lay in Jordan's arms, content as she'd ever been, until sleep claimed them.

When she came awake, she was surprised to see sunlight streaming through her bedroom windows, but the bed beside her was empty.

Frowning, she looked around the room, but then heard sounds from the kitchen. She cleaned up in the bathroom, donned some sweats and pulled her hair into a messy ponytail before padding out to find Jordan.

He was in the kitchen—at the stove, no less. She let a mix of emotions pass over her—pleasure and, yes, worry. Had she never fully shucked her fears about being disappointed by a man after Neil?

"Hey, sexy." Jordan held a spatula in his hand, and mouthwatering aromas filled the kitchen.

"Back at you."

Sera eyed him; he was tousled and edible-looking. He'd donned last night's suit pants but otherwise he was bare-chested—all rippling, lean muscle. Sera drank in the view of what was covered up during therapy.

Jordan smiled at her. "Hungry?"

How could he be so cheery so soon after sunrise? Okay, the sex had been spectacular. She felt like a well-sated cat. But still, mornings were mornings. She yawned and moved toward a cabinet to pull down a coffee mug.

"You know, I once asked if the clouds ever come out in Serenghetti Land," she muttered. "I guess the answer is no."

Jordan laughed. "Angel, I'm guessing I'll always need to be the one in charge of breakfast for us."

Retrieving her mug, she answered, "You got that right."

And then she realized...*always?* She hadn't blinked at his allusion to a next time—more than one, in fact—for them. She tested the idea and registered that it made her...happy. Butterflies-in-the-stomach happy, actually. Last night, her relationship with Jordan had taken a big step toward *complicated*, but right now, she wanted to shut out the world for a little bit longer and just experience the moment.

"Grumpy in the morning?"

"Yes." *Well, until seconds ago, anyway.* She poured herself a cup of dark brew that he'd had ready for her.

"I'll file that information away for future reference."

"I bet you've always dated the kind of woman who sleeps in her makeup so she can wake up camera-ready," she grumbled before savoring her first sip of coffee.

Jordan just smiled again. "Don't worry. You're cute in the morning—"

"Only in the morning?"

"—in a tussled-in-the-sheets kind of way."

"Hmm." *Thanks to him.* She looked at the stove. "What are you making?"

"The Serenghetti Brothers Frittata."

"So you do cook."

"Breakfast, sometimes. I think I mentioned it before. Since I often slept in, it was the one meal where Mom wasn't ruling the kitchen."

"Late-night carousing, I bet. I'm guessing you were having a lot of breakfasts later than everyone else. Closer to noon, maybe?"

He tossed her a meaningful look. "I'm not going to incriminate myself."

"Of course."

"When I started living on my own, making breakfast became a survival skill."

"Along with getting the right meal partner?"

"Jealous?"

"Please."

He looked boyishly charmed by her denial. "Something tells me you're going to be my best…meal partner ever."

"Oh?" She kept her tone casual. "Well, you're about to find out."

In fact, his frittata was delicious. And afterward, not least because it was her kitchen, she took charge of cleanup, while he headed to the shower. Wiping down the kitchen counter minutes later, she heard the water running and gave in to the urge she'd been resisting since she woke up.

She stripped off her clothes and headed in the direction of the running water.

Opening the bathroom door, she could see him in the shower stall. He held a disposable razor in one hand and one of her cosmetic mirrors with the other. As he shaved, she slipped up behind him and rested her hands on his hips and her cheek on his back.

When he reached for the shampoo, she stopped him and instead poured a dollop into the palm of her hand and went to work massaging his hair.

He tilted his head back in order to help her reach. And after several moments, he said, "Ah, Sera. Are we going for round two here?"

"Feels good?" she murmured.

"Feels great."

"Mmm." She could feel her body humming and vibrating to life.

"How about you go to work on the ache that's flared up?"

Her brow puckered. "Your knee is bothering you?"

"Right now, I could use your hands on me, Angel."

Concerned, she rinsed the suds from his hair and then bent down to place her hands on his knee.

Laughing, Jordan grasped her arm and pulled her up and around to face him.

Immediately, she realized he was aroused. "I thought you said your knee injury was bothering you."

He gave her a quick peck on the lips. "I didn't mention my knee, but I'm aching in other ways."

She realized she felt the same.

When had she started agreeing with him?

Eleven

Jordan couldn't stop thinking about her. He'd always stuck to casual relationships. What was the saying about best-laid plans?

The sex…it had been fantastic. Mind-blowing, even though that sounded trite. She'd been so responsive, and he'd been able to relieve a sexual frustration that had gone on forever—building up to the breaking point at his cousin's wedding, of all places. Not that he felt relief—now he itched to spend every moment with her.

He'd fantasized about her last night, reliving their evening together, except he'd woken aroused…and to an empty bed. Still, the memories had been vivid. The way she'd looked at the moment of her release—her back arched, her breath coming audibly between parted lips, her eyes half-closed.

Jordan almost groaned aloud, shifted on the bar stool and tightened his grip on his beer. He took a deep breath. If he wasn't careful, he'd embarrass himself or race to find Sera.

Usually weddings like the one the other day were a reminder that he wasn't looking to make a serious commitment himself. He liked his life just fine. At his cousin's ceremony, though, every thought had fallen by the wayside except getting closer to the woman he'd wanted to seduce.

He was pensive this evening even though he'd come to the Puck & Shoot to relax. He couldn't even manage more than distracted conversation with Vince, who occupied the next stool.

On days like today, he had to wonder whether the whole sports celebrity gig was worth it. Because, on top of it, while he'd gotten a reprieve from the press during the off-season and because he was out of commission with a bad knee, lately they'd acted up again.

"Serenghetti." Marc Bellitti slapped him on the back as he walked up. "It's good to see you nearly looking like your old self."

"Yup." Jordan took a swig of his beer.

"Sera must be miracle worker." Marc flashed a grin. "She almost makes me want to have a bum knee."

Jordan's hand tightened on his drink again—because he had a sudden inexplicable urge to get in Marc's face. Once, not so long ago, he'd been like his teammate—unable to remember names, but always able to recall a pretty face and a body to match. But things had changed. *He'd* changed. Maybe it was the injury, maybe it was Sera, maybe it was the two together. After all, he had her to thank for his amazing recovery.

Marc propped his forearm against the bar. "You haven't even glanced at the blonde at table six throwing hot-and-heavy looks your way. So I have to say you're only *nearly* back to normal."

Jordan glanced over his shoulder. "She's not my type."

"Serenghetti, they're all your type. What's wrong with her?"

"Too young."

Marc gave a mock gasp and clutched his chest. "Be still my heart. You cruised past thirty, and suddenly twenty-five is too young?"

"How do you know how old she is?"

Marc gave a sly smile. "On my way over here to keep company with your sorry cooking-competition-losing self, I happened to find out she's already got her degree and is going for another in marine biology."

"As I said, not my type."

"Well, well," Marc drawled, "look which kitty cat has changed his stripes."

Vince laughed.

"Maybe you're still thinking about that physical therapist," Marc commented.

"Appearances can be deceiving," Jordan responded, refusing to be drawn in.

He'd rather eat a hockey puck or two than admit to...*feelings*. He'd never hear the end of it from his teammates.

"Meaning?" Marc prompted.

Jordan raised his eyebrows but made sure to keep

his tone nonchalant. "Maybe Sera's just my biggest challenge yet."

Or he was hers. Damn. He and Sera had never discussed the future, and he'd been content to live in the moment. *And what moments they'd been...* Still, the last thing he needed was for his teammates to latch onto the idea that his relationship with Sera was anything more than casual. Although, how he and Sera were going to continue to keep things on the down low after shattering the final barrier in their relationship on the night of his cousin's wedding, he had no idea. Sera hadn't said anything, but they were already skating on thin ice with Mia in the know.

"What about our bet that you could make her melt?" Marc asked. "Are you conceding defeat?" His teammate tut-tutted. "You're on a losing streak, Serenghetti. First, the cooking show, now—"

"I'm not conceding anything." Jordan made a motion indicating he was zipping his lips and throwing away the key. Let Marc speculate all he wanted. He wasn't going to admit anything—or divulge intimate details.

When Marc just laughed, Jordan glanced over his shoulder and then sobered. "Hi, Dante."

He wondered how long Sera's brother had been standing there and what he'd heard and then shrugged off the thought. His words could be read in many ways.

She'd never felt this way about a guy. There, she'd admitted it. He'd been a laundry list of her *nevers*, but Jordan had somehow become her *must-have*. She couldn't wait to see him again, jump his bones and float in a happy bubble of coupledom.

Her former self would have found it all ridiculously saccharine instead of cause for a goofy smile. Few would be able to tolerate her right now—even her own past selves.

Take Marisa, for example.

She'd just run into her cousin in the produce aisle of the local supermarket, Bellerose. Pushing her cart and daydreaming, she'd almost jumped when Marisa had called out her name.

Her cousin knit her brow. "Are you okay?"

"Just peachy," Sera managed, even though all she wanted to do was throw her arms wide and twirl. In the middle of the produce aisle. "It's been ages since I've run into you here."

"That's because I'm normally trapped in the baby aisle comparing package labels and feeling guilty about not pureeing everything myself," Marisa quipped and then tucked a stray strand behind her ear. "These days, if I manage to get out of the house without spit-up on my shirt, I'm good."

Sera smiled. "And where is the marvelous Dahlia?"

"At home with Daddy and, with any luck, napping. Cole had the day off."

As they continued to chat, lingering in the aisle, Sera shifted from one foot to another.

She knew her cousin had to be full of speculation about her appearance on Jordan's arm at the wedding. Plus, this was no longer simply one amorous encounter with Jordan that she'd told him to swear to take to the grave. Any last shred of professional distance was gone. She and Jordan had done the deed, and short of amnesia, she was never likely to forget that night—in all its pyrotechnic glory.

As if on cue, Marisa said, "So how is Jordan these days?"

Sera made herself shrug nonchalantly. "He's been recovering nicely."

"Mmm-hmm." Her cousin looked amused. "He seems to be in great shape. Enough to attend a wedding."

With you as his date. The unspoken words hung in the air.

"I went with him because it got me out of giving Jordan the cooking lesson that his mom suggested," Sera blurted and then could have bitten off her tongue. There was no need to clarify why she'd been with Jordan, and being defensive definitely made it seem like a date. Her face heated.

"Mmm-hmm."

"Will you stop saying that?"

Marisa smiled. "Please. The guy's been tracking you with his eyes."

Sera felt a hot wave of embarrassment. "I didn't even want to be his physical therapist. I tried to get myself out of it."

"Yeah, but the attraction was so strong, maybe you were just afraid to go there."

Sera bit her lip. *Afraid.* She hadn't given more than a passing thought to Neil in…it was probably a new record. Instead, her mind—and heart—had been consumed by Jordan. She supposed it was all a sign of how far she'd come since her bad breakup. Sure, she'd had boyfriends before, but nothing serious until Neil—or so she'd thought. But her relationship with Neil had been skating on the surface in comparison to the depths she'd plunged into with Jordan.

Jordan had wrung every emotion out of her—annoyance, exasperation, nervousness, need, hunger, joy, pleasure. It was like living life in an explosion of color, especially in bed.

Just then, another shopper came by, and Sera and Marisa separated in order to let the older woman through with her cart. Sera took the opportunity to glance at her watch to try to extricate herself from this tricky conversation. If she lingered, she expected more gentle probing and teasing.

But her cousin just winked at her. "Keep me posted."

Sera rolled her eyes. "Right."

Saying goodbye to Marisa with a promise to catch up another time, she headed to the checkout line.

Minutes later, after she'd loaded the groceries into her car and had gotten behind the wheel, her cell phone rang. Noticing it was from Dante, she turned off the ignition and took the call.

After a brief exchange, during which Sera wondered why Dante was calling, her brother asked, "How are things going with you and Jordan?"

"Great." The trending topic of the day: #JordanandSera.

Dante cleared his throat. "Just be careful."

"Don't worry," she replied, hoping to keep this conversation light,. "I promise not to let him break a bone on all that physical-therapy equipment." She hadn't confided in her brother about her true relationship status with Jordan these days, so she wondered what her brother was getting at. Unless Mia had been loose-lipped, despite her promise to button it? Sera tightened her hold on her cell. "Is there anything you're not telling me?"

"No. Yes. I heard you went as his date to a family wedding."

"I did. He needed one. He's injured…and not getting around much." It wasn't a total lie, but she added quickly, "I didn't mention it to you or Mom because it was casual." *And I didn't want you to make too much of it.*

There was a pause. "I know I'm going to regret this, but my loyalty to my little sister is bigger—"

"Than what?"

"I ran into Jordan at the Puck & Shoot."

Sera forced nonchalance. "And so? He was flirting with Angus?"

"You know Angus has been married fifty years."

"Thirty-five."

"Who's counting?"

"He is. When he skipped over his wedding anniversary two years ago, his wife never let him forget it."

"No, Angus is out of the picture. But listen, I overheard Jordan joking with some Razors about you being his biggest challenge yet."

Well, she was. Or did Jordan mean she was just another conquest? It was an ambiguous statement, but the fact that he'd been joking with his teammates when he'd said it wasn't a good sign.

"Right before that, I heard Jordan tell Marc Bellitti that appearances can be deceiving."

Hadn't she thought the same thing about Jordan recently? She'd discovered he volunteered with a children's charity. And she'd been basking in the realization that he wasn't quite the player she'd thought he was. "In what context did he say this?"

"To be honest, Marc was ragging Jordan about being hung up on you."

Even Jordan's teammates were onto them? She strove to keep her voice neutral—bored even. "I've been a waitress at the Puck & Shoot. I've heard it all. They were probably just shooting the breeze."

"Jordan and Matt had a bet—"

"Players often do."

"—that he couldn't seduce you. Or, uh, to be more precise, make you 'melt.'"

She froze. It was like Shakespeare's *The Taming of the Shrew*, and she knew what her role was. Her lips tightened. Yes, she was pissed off. But she was going to hold her fire and question Jordan at the appropriate time. Have him explain himself. *If he could.*

She sighed, conceding her brother's good intentions in telling her all this. "Thanks, Dante." She watched a cloud pass in front of the sun, darkening the inside of her car. "I owe you." *Poor Sera, saved by her family again.*

Surprisingly, though, she didn't get an immediate wisecrack from Dante. Instead, her brother matched her tone of resignation. "What are siblings for? Anyway, these days, you've been coming to my aid just as much. More, actually."

Dante's words were almost enough to bring a smile

to her face. Because he was right—and there was the small silver lining to her current predicament.

She was a mature and intelligent woman. Or so Sera kept reminding herself.

In the days since speaking with her brother, she'd come up with a plan—once she was done being miffed. She was willing to give Jordan the benefit of the doubt. After all, she'd witnessed plenty of ribbing banter while waitressing at the Puck & Shoot, just as she'd told Dante. The best strategy might be to beat Jordan and his buddies at their own game.

Could it have been only a week since Constance and Oliver's wedding? So much had happened, including the buildup of sexual frustration. Work and other commitments had kept her and Jordan apart except for physical therapy, and then Dante's news had led her to bide her time until tonight, when Jordan had suggested dinner out at Altavista.

She and Jordan had been served wine but had yet to order their meal. *Time to have a little fun.*

She leaned close, drawing Jordan's attention, so she could keep her voice low. "I've been thinking all week about Saturday night."

Jordan's eyes kindled. "What a coincidence. So have I."

"Hmm." *And not just so he could claim to have won a stupid bet?*

"I don't want to rush you, but, yeah—" the corner of his mouth turned up "—I've wanted a repeat."

She dipped the top of her finger into the top of her

wineglass and then, without breaking eye contact, brought that finger to her lips.

Jordan swallowed, his throat working.

She knew him well enough now to recognize the flare of arousal. They occupied a cozy corner table for two, where they could engage in semipublic flirtation without attracting too much attention. She wanted to have some fun while she made him eat his words.

Deliberately, she let her leg brush against his. Her wrap dress clung to her breasts, and she leaned forward, knowing her cleavage would be on full display. "I want to make you melt."

"Sera," he said in a low voice, his gaze kindling, "the appetizer hasn't even arrived, and you're—"

"Ready for dessert?" She trailed the wine-stained finger from her collarbone to the swell of her breasts.

Jordan cleared his throat and lowered his eyes to follow the motion of her finger.

"I came straight from work. I'm a little…breathless."

He lifted his gaze then and fixed it on her. "You're wearing clingy dresses in your therapy sessions these days? For which client?"

She gave a throaty laugh. "Don't be silly. I changed into my thong and dress in the bathroom before I drove over here."

Jordan sucked in a breath. "You're playing with me, aren't you?"

Yes, she was enjoying turning the tables.

"I don't know what's put you in this mood—"

"Well, it's been a while since we've had sex. Now that I've had a taste, I want more."

He groaned, and she gave him a naughty smile.

Jordan thrust his crumpled napkin onto the table. "That's it. Let's go. I'll leave a big tip for the wine we ordered and for the meal we didn't."

"But we haven't had dinner."

His gaze was hot on her face. "We'll order in. After."

"Jordan," she murmured, "you look a little flushed. Are you hot?"

"Yeah, for you," he growled back, waving away an approaching waiter. "Great invitation, by the way. I accept."

She curved her lips and then shifted in her seat. She took a large swallow from her water glass to steady herself and then regarded him over the rim.

"Sera." There was an edge to his voice. "We need to leave now. Otherwise I won't be able to without—"

"Mmm. Wouldn't want your teammates to see that, would we?"

"Exactly."

"After all, you're the one who's supposed to make me melt."

Jordan stilled and then groaned again. Except this time, the sound was self-deprecating.

Sera tilted her head and regarded him.

"I can explain."

"I'm sure. I can't wait to hear it."

"Who told you? Dante?" he said on an exhale. "Sera, it was a ridiculous bet—"

"At my expense."

"And a flippant remark—"

"To uphold the great and mighty Jordan Serenghetti reputation?"

"Damn it."

"Amen."

"Are you going to make me grovel?"

"Or at least work for it," she replied teasingly. "Let me help you out here. 'I was just being one of the guys.'"

"Check."

"'We don't wear emotion well.'"

"Check."

"'It was false male bravado. Psych 101.'"

"Check again." He took her hand. "I'll take it from here. I'm frustrated about not being on the ice. Getting grief about you from my teammates was heaping—"

"Insult onto injury?" she asked drolly.

He looked sheepish. "Yeah. I didn't want to go there with them...about you. Because it was you, and you're special."

"I'm going to have to get tough with the Razors crew."

Jordan smiled. "They already know you can kick ass on TV."

"Mmm-hmm."

He lifted her hand and kissed her knuckles. "Forgiven?"

"I ought to make you take cooking lessons live for a season."

Jordan shuddered. "Please. The last episode nearly did me in." Then he sobered. "Anyway, this isn't about some asinine bet or tit for tat. The truth is I've lost track of which one of us owes a favor to the other. Because somewhere along the way, I stopped caring. Except about being with you."

Wow. She wanted to believe those words. His bet had

cast doubt on what she'd thought was something genuine and true and beautiful. She still had faith in him, but it had been nicked. But then, she hadn't expected him to crack open with emotional honesty tonight.

"I had this germ of a plan to make a major donation to Welsdale Children's Hospital," Jordan went on after a pause. "Thanks to you, I might still have a career that'll make that possible."

She blinked.

"It'll be a hospital addition for rehabilitation facilities. Because I understand how important physical therapy is."

Sera parted her lips on an indrawn breath. She'd started out annoyed and ready to teach him a lesson, but somehow they'd ended up in a place where he held her heart.

Jordan caressed the back of her hand with his thumb. "I have a meeting with hospital management in the next few weeks. I'd like you to be there."

She blinked again. It wasn't a marriage proposal, but this was heady stuff. He was asking her to weigh in on a major life decision—one that would involve millions of dollars. "Why?"

"You'll have a perspective on things that I won't. I value your opinion." He gave a lopsided smile. "You're important to me."

His words were sexier than any underwear billboard. On impulse, she cupped his face and kissed him, heedless of the other diners scattered through the dim restaurant.

When she sat back, Jordan laughed.

"Hey," he said, "I wasn't joking earlier when I said

we needed to get out of here fast. Any more PDAs and—"

"—we'll be putting on an R-rated performance?"

"Anyone ever tell you that you have a knack for finishing my sentences?"

"We're on the same wavelength."

"That's not all I'd like to be," Jordan growled.

"Get the check, Serenghetti."

Twelve

By the time he and Sera arrived back at his place, it was all Jordan could do to hold himself in check until they stepped off the elevator inside his apartment.

"This place is different than I remember," she remarked. "But then, I was a little shaken up after the accident and maybe not picking up the same details."

He was shaken up *now*. He kissed the back of her neck and let his hands roam up her body.

He wanted to make love to her again. It was a need he hadn't experienced this sharply...ever.

She'd surprised him with her reaction to the ridiculous challenge he'd taken up with Marc. Another woman might have given him the silent treatment and left him to guess why.

But Sera had...attitude. She drove him crazy and made him ache with need.

Even in his sleep, he could taste her and inhale her scent. And ever since their encounter after the wedding, he's been itching to get her alone. He'd meant it when he said all he could think about these days was being with her.

When they got to his bedroom, he turned her around to face him and kissed her. She met him with a longing of her own, her mouth tangling with his.

He pulled at the tie at her waist and her dress fell open. He drank her in with his eyes. "You're a fantasy come true, Sera."

They kissed again, and he inched her in the direction of his bed. Within a few steps, her dress fell to the floor, followed by his shirt.

He cupped her breasts, feeling their luxurious weight and letting his thumbs move over the twin peaks covered by the thin fabric of her bra.

"Do you like my hands on you?" he murmured.

"Yesss." Her breath was shallow and rapid, her pupils dilated.

He wanted her to feel the depth of his need and reciprocate it. He wanted to bring her pleasure.

Sliding his hands under her arms, he unhooked her bra at the back and watched those glorious breasts spill against him.

Then holding her gaze, he bent and gave attention to each breast with his mouth.

She moaned, and her fingers tangled in his hair. "Jordan…"

He closed his eyes, focusing on drawing one peak into his mouth and then the other.

Sera's knees bent, and she leaned in to him.

Yes. He told her all the things he wanted to do with her, until her breath came in rapid rasps. Her skin tasted flowery, making him want her all the more.

When he straightened, his hand went to the juncture of her thighs. "You are so ready for me, Angel."

She had a half-lidded look, her color heightened, her lips red.

"It's going to be so good. I've been waiting for days for a repeat."

She wet her lips and then stroked her hand up and down his erection. "Please."

He breathed deep. "What do you want?"

In response, she surprised him by undoing his belt and stripping him out of his pants. She pressed kisses to his bare chest, making him groan. And then she stroked him with a sure hand, bringing him ever closer to the brink.

"Ah, Sera."

She bent before him and took him in her mouth, loving him.

Jordan's eyes closed on a wave of pleasure. When he couldn't take anymore—knowing he was unbearably close—he tugged her up and stripped her underwear from her.

She lay back on the beige comforter covering his bed, her hair splayed around her.

Jordan fumbled with some protection from a nearby dresser drawer and then braced himself over her.

Holding her gaze as her legs came around him, he sheathed himself inside her, and they both sighed.

Jordan gritted his teeth. "You're so damn hot and tight. So good."

He began to move, and she met him stroke for stroke. Jordan closed his eyes, intent on drawing out the interlude. Within minutes, however, it was too much for both of them.

Sera lifted her hips and arched her back with her climax, and watching her glorious reaction, Jordan came apart himself, his hoarse groan a testament to reaching a new peak.

Afterward, he slumped against her and gathered her to him, and they were both content to let sleep claim them.

Sera reflected that the only word that could sum up the past week or so was *idyllic*. She and Jordan had snuck away to spend a weekend at a cozy bungalow he had on Cape Cod, taking a balloon ride over the wooded fields and overall enjoying living in their own new and kaleidoscopic little world.

Now as she and Jordan arrived hand in hand at a local movie theater near Welsdale, Sera found herself both content to enjoy the evening and bursting with plans for their burgeoning relationship. Jordan's recovery was going so well, soon they'd be able to head to the boxing gym together. And in future outings to Cape Cod, they could water-ski, take a boat out on the water and even go parasailing. Jordan had dared her to try the last.

"Jordan, Jordan!"

The paparazzo came out of nowhere, camera flashing like a firearm. Sera bent her head down as she and Jordan headed toward the doors of the theater. So far, they'd been able to duck photographers despite his celebrity. Probably the fact that it was the off-season and he'd been convalescing helped.

Sera didn't delude herself, however, that their honeymoon would last forever. Jordan was too well-known. And while they'd been able to keep their relationship under wraps until recently even from their families, this photographer meant she'd have to figure out fast how to deal with being outed. The fact that she and Jordan were holding hands was a giveaway that they were more than casual acquaintances.

As the photographer snapped away, he also jogged to catch up to them. "Any comment on the news report?"

"Whatever it is, the answer is no," Jordan tossed back.

"Are you denying that you're the father of Lauren Zummen's child?"

Sera stiffened and swung her gaze to Jordan, whose expression had turned grim.

"Anything you want to say?"

"Again, no."

In the next moment, Jordan changed course and was hustling her back to his car—obviously trying to shake the paparazzo.

"No denial?" the photographer called out after them.

"How did you know where we were?" Jordan asked, not looking behind him.

"I have my sources." The paparazzo sounded cheery.

Stunned, Sera silently followed Jordan. Suddenly, what their families might think of their relationship was the least of her problems. And her concern about the stupid bet he'd made with his teammates seemed laughable in comparison.

They both said nothing as they got into the car and Jordan pulled away from the curb, leaving their pursuer far behind them. Obviously, a night out couldn't happen now. They'd be sitting ducks for more unwanted attention.

Sera felt a roaring in her ears. Finally, she forced herself to say, "Do you know what he was talking about?"

She could tell from Jordan's face that he had some inkling at least—and he'd chosen to say nothing to her about it.

"There are rumors…"

She gripped her handbag, pressing her knuckles into the folds. She could've heard those rumors at any time and would have been unprepared to deal with them. She was unprepared to deal with them *now*. "Where are we going?"

"Back to your place because it's closer, so we can talk. Privately."

She took his words as confirmation of her worst suspicions and briefly closed her eyes. "So there's a baby?"

Jordan nodded, not taking his eyes off the road.

"Did you know the mother?" She felt as if she was chewing sawdust as she said it.

"The first time I heard her last name attached to the rumors is when the photographer just said it. Yes, I knew her. But once and for a short time."

"Once is all it takes, isn't it?" she retorted.

This time, he did glance at her. "There's no proof that I'm the father."

"And there's nothing to say you're not."

Jordan hit his palm against the steering wheel. "You're asking me to prove a negative when I haven't even taken a paternity test."

How could this be happening to her again? Was she a marked woman? She'd now dated *two* men who'd had families—children—she hadn't known about. For the second time, she'd experienced the most brutal deception.

"Sera, those kinds of accusations are not that uncommon for professional athletes."

She knew what he was saying. Sports stars were targets for fortune hunters. Her own cousin Marisa was the product of a pro athlete's short-term liaison, though Aunt Donna hadn't asked for or received a penny from Marisa's father, whose minor-league baseball dreams had died along with him in a freak accident.

"The story is that the girl is two and a half," Jordan said quietly.

"When are you going to take a paternity test?"

He didn't take his eyes off the road—didn't glance at her. "This allegation has come out of the blue. I need to have Marv, my agent, arrange to investigate it."

"Why didn't you tell me?"

"I figured it was baseless gossip until now. I want to have the facts first."

Right. Time to figure out how to spin this story for her, perhaps? There was always a reason—an explanation. Neil had had one, too.

When they arrived at her apartment, she popped

out of the car and shot for the door. She heard his car door slam and then Jordan rushing to catch up to her.

"Sera!"

She didn't want to talk about this right now. How could she be so stupid? *Again.*

She must be giving some kind of signal to men: *this one is easy to dupe.*

Jordan touched her arm, and she spun toward him. "Leave me alone."

"We need to talk. Listen—"

"No, you listen." She stabbed a finger in the direction of his chest. "I don't like being had."

He had the indecency to appear surprised. "Neither do I."

"There's a lot about you I apparently didn't know."

"Let's talk somewhere more private."

"I don't think so." No way was she continuing this… *discussion.* Especially inside her apartment. So he could work his *charm* on her and *gaslight* her. There'd be nowhere to run if she was completely broken.

Neil had played with her mind, too. And her feelings—and her heart. *You've got it all wrong, Sera… My marriage isn't real… I adore you.* Afterward, she'd discovered at the bar where she'd first met him that he'd been a longtime customer, and she hadn't been the first woman he'd dallied with. And there'd been a baby, all right—or at least a toddler. A two-year-old who'd lived with his wife in Boston.

Jordan remained silent but sighed and shoved his hands in his pockets.

"What? Nothing to say? This news didn't come as a complete surprise to you."

"I told you what I know. It was sudden, and I just learned the mother's last name. I'm still processing it."

"How stupid do you think I am? These types of scandals are usually percolating for a while before they grab a lot of headlines. And you—" she sucked in a deep breath "—didn't tell me."

"I didn't think you'd be this upset that I'd waited."

"What?" She stared at him. "I wouldn't be upset that you're a father, and I didn't know it?"

"Alleged father. And I recently found out myself."

"But you knew before tonight." She made a strangled sound and then muttered, "I should have learned my lesson with Neil."

"Who's Neil?"

"The guy I had the misfortune to date after he walked into my bar." She paused. "Until I discovered he was married and had a wife and toddler daughter squirreled away in Boston." Her voice dripped sarcasm. "Conveniently far but not too far away from Welsdale, where he traveled frequently on business."

Jordan swore.

Sera gave a humorless laugh. "To think that I thought my biggest problem with you was some ridiculous bet that you'd made with Marc Bellitti about—" she waved her hand "—making me melt. I guess we all know who the fool is, don't we?"

Jordan looked solemn. "Sera… I'm sorry."

"Yes, I guess there's nothing else to say, is there?" she replied flippantly, feeling traitorous tears welling. "Except sometimes *I'm sorry* isn't enough. Goodbye, Jordan."

* * *

Jordan stared broodingly at his apartment wall from his spot on the sofa.

When he'd reluctantly driven off earlier without settling things with Sera, he realized that he needed the truth first before he could convince her. Had he really fathered a child he hadn't known about? He'd always been careful. In this case, more than three years ago, he'd been intimate with Lauren once, and he'd used protection. Sure, such measures weren't foolproof, but it gave him reason to question the veracity of the claims here.

He'd met Lauren at a party, and she'd come on strong. She'd had a summer-vacation share on Cape Cod with a bunch of twentysomethings—and his house had been nearby. He'd quickly realized they didn't have much in common, so he'd let her down easy and had never seen or heard from her again. Until now.

Sure, those minimal facts would be small consolation to Sera. But he also wasn't the same person he'd been three years ago. These days, an aspiring groupie held little appeal for him.

He knew what he had to do. If he was already being stalked by paparazzi, the story was spreading quickly. He couldn't afford to wait, even if his agent had flagged the story for him just yesterday—as he often did when his name popped up online, associated with good or negative articles. He'd have to tell his family before they read about it. *Before they had a reaction of shock and disappoint akin to Sera's.*

He winced inwardly. First, though, he had to mar-shal his resources.

Picking up the phone, he called Marv.

His agent answered on the third ring, sounding sleepy.

"Early bedtime these days, Marv?" Jordan couldn't resist teasing.

"What's up?" Marvin replied in a gravelly voice.

Jordan sobered. "I need you to follow up on the re-cent gossip story about the baby I allegedly fathered. I can't afford to wait, and we need to move up the time-line about how we react."

"What happened?"

"A paparazzo caught up with me tonight, and the story is gaining traction." He paused, tightening his jaw. "He blurted the woman's last name, and I just discovered that this Lauren is someone I may have known."

He didn't need to spell things out for Marv. Lauren was a common enough name that it had been easy for both him and his agent to initially dismiss this story. But now he was admitting to Marv that this was a woman from his past. And Jordan knew he had to face the consequences, one way or another. "I'm willing to take a paternity test if necessary."

What if he was the father? He weighed the idea. Sure, he figured he'd have kids someday. He liked kids. He loved being the newly minted uncle to his broth-ers' babies. He cared enough to fund-raise with Once upon a Dream and want to sponsor new facilities at Children's Hospital. But having children of his own wasn't something he'd seriously contemplated up to now given his lifestyle; he was at the peak of his career. Plus, if he was honest, he'd say he'd never met a woman he wanted to have kids with.

An image of Sera flashed through his mind, and he started to smile. His baby and Sera's would be a firecracker, no question.

Marv sighed. "You know, a scandal on top of everything else won't be good for the revenue stream or your contract-negotiating position. I gotta put that out there."

"We're living in the era of reality-TV stars. Don't be too sure," Jordan responded drily. "Anyway, I want the truth—whatever it is."

"Of course."

"I want you to hire a private investigator and find out all you can. I need as much background as possible fast."

He trusted Marv and considered him more than an agent because of their long-standing working relationship. That was why he was asking him to be the point person and hire whomever and do whatever it took.

"You got it," his agent said. "And Jordan?"

"Yeah?"

"No matter what the truth is, you can handle it."

"Thanks for the vote of confidence, Marv."

His life had been turned upside down, but he'd been in worse situations before.

Thirteen

"Bernice, I need to be reassigned."

Sera stood in the doorway of her manager's office, not looking at Bernice but focused on the bobblehead dolls on the shelves. Frankly, she felt a bit like a bobblehead herself lately.

It wasn't every day that a woman had to deal with being outed as a couple in the press and a private breakup *at the same time*. From some angles, it would seem that she and Jordan had the shortest relationship on record. They were the local version of a Las Vegas wedding *and* divorce.

Plus, the juiciness of Jordan being outed as a baby daddy while dating another woman at the same time was making the press slaver.

The twin headlines ran through her head: "Jordan

Serenghetti's Secret Love Child." "Jordan Serenghetti's New Mystery Woman."

Bernice swiveled her chair so that she faced Sera more fully. "You want to be reassigned? Because Jordan may have fathered a child?"

"You know already?"

"Honey, everyone knows. It's Jordan Serenghetti. The news is hard to avoid, especially around here, and I'm not a good gossip-dodger."

Sera wasn't ashamed to admit she'd cried last night. The pain had been a dull throb in the region of her heart. If it had been sharp and awful but over and done within minutes, she might have been thankful. Instead, she had this agonizing aftermath.

It wasn't as if she'd be able to avoid Jordan for the rest of her life. Not unless she declined Marisa and Cole's future invites. And maybe not entirely even then. Welsdale wasn't that big a town, and she was bound to run into Jordan eventually, even if she ducked every event that Marisa and Cole planned for Dahlia or any other child they might have.

Which brought Sera back to the children she and Jordan would never have. Because he may have already plunged into parenthood with another woman, and had hidden it from her—just like Neil had.

Why hadn't she learned? Her inner voice wailed and raged, refusing to be silenced.

Bernice looked at her sympathetically.

"I know you said we need this contract with the Razors..." Sera trailed off and bit her trembling lip. Damn it. *She would not cry.* She'd thought she'd used up all her tears last night.

"Things got a little too cozy with Jordan?"

Sera nodded, still avoiding her manager's gaze. She'd behaved unprofessionally—she inwardly rolled her eyes—and with Jordan Serenghetti, of all people. He was an in-law and a sports celebrity.

"Feelings?"

"Yeah," she responded thickly.

She blamed Jordan—and herself. How had she fallen prey to his charm? She should have known better. She did know better. And even if she had to keep banging her head against a wall, she *would* do better next time.

Bernice sighed. "The smooth-as-honey jocks are always the ones that are hardest to resist."

"You know?" Sera raised her eyebrows. Bernice seemed to be speaking from experience.

"Remind me to tell you about Miguel another time."

Sera's eyes widened because her manager had been married for years. Had Bernice had an affair?

"He was pre-Keith," her manager added. "I learned my lesson."

Sera wished she had, too.

"Okay," Bernice said briskly. "When's your next appointment with the Razors' resident bad boy?"

"Wednesday at two."

"Let me look at my schedule and see who else on staff is available."

Sera relaxed her shoulders. "Thanks, Bernice."

"We can tell him you're unavailable this week and work from there, until this situation gets resolved."

As far as Sera was concerned, this situation was already resolved. She and Jordan were over and done.

She shook her head. "This isn't a temporary squabble. There's no hope—"

Bernice waved her hand. "We'll see."

Sera sighed. At least she had a temporary reprieve. "Thanks, Bernice."

Sera did her best to focus on work for the rest of the day. On the way home, she stopped at Bellerose in order to pick up some groceries. She was either going to cook and bake her troubles away or indulge in some premade comfort food—maybe both.

On the way to the ice-cream section, she stopped abruptly as she caught sight of her cousin Marisa—or rather, her cousin spotted her. She bit back a groan.

"We have to stop meeting this way," Marisa joked, maneuvering her cart out of the way.

Tell me about it. The last thing she needed right now was to run into her cousin. She wasn't sure she had time to put on her *brave face.* "Let me guess. With Dahlia around now, you mostly get to do the supermarket run only in the evenings when Cole gets home."

Her cousin smiled. "Bingo."

Unfortunately, Sera thought, it was also the time when she'd be getting out of work and maybe stopping for milk on the way home. Karma was against her these days in a major way.

Marisa searched her cousin's face and then glanced around them as if to be sure they had some privacy for the moment. "How are you doing?"

"As well as can be expected today," Sera responded noncommittally.

"I was going to call you later on, after I knew you'd

be home from work. If you need someone to lend an ear or a shoulder..."

Sera blinked. "To cry on?" She shrugged. "Sorry, all my tears have been washed away."

Marisa sighed.

"How are the Serenghettis handling the news?" Sera damned herself for asking.

After she and Jordan had been ambushed by the photographer, she'd figured it was just a matter of time until the news became really public—though she hadn't expected it to find its way to Bernice so quickly. Perhaps Jordan had called to forewarn his family...a courtesy he hadn't extended to her. Maybe he'd learned something from her reaction to being caught by surprise and decided telling others himself was the better course.

"Jordan has told all of us that he doesn't know what's true yet."

Sera shrugged again. "Well, best of luck to him."

Marisa looked worried. "Oh, Sera, I know you care."

"Do you?"

"I thought, especially at the wedding, that there was a special spark between you and Jordan." Marisa searched her expression again. "Was I wrong?"

"Does it matter now? The only thing that does is that I was a fool. Again."

"Because Jordan may have a child?"

"Because he didn't tell me!" Sera waved a hand. "Like a certain lying ex-boyfriend. I seem to have a special gift for ferreting out impostors."

"Oh, I don't know, the feelings between you seemed very real to me."

As another customer turned into their aisle, they moved apart.

"I need to go," Sera said quickly. "Before someone recognizes me from the news."

"I'm here if you need me."

Sera just nodded as she moved down the aisle, but she mulled over Marisa's words.

Feelings. The magic word. First Bernice, now her cousin. She was hoping these *feelings* would go away soon. Far, far away.

Fool. Sera had called herself the dirty word more times than she could count in the past few days. What kind of pushover got taken for a ride twice by men singing the same tune? Would she ever learn?

She'd taken to the gym with a vengeance. Pilates, yoga, kickboxing, two-mile runs. There was no hurdle that she wouldn't surmount. But she couldn't overcome her fury. Okay, her pain.

Damn it.

And now she was facing Sunday dinner with her family at her mother's house. Not showing up wasn't an option. Her family would just take her absence as confirmation that something was amiss—and perhaps wonder and worry more than they already were. She had to face reality, and the sooner the better.

After serving the spaghetti and meatballs, her mother eyed her speculatively. "I heard the most outrageous story this week. I knew it couldn't possibly be true."

"Hmm." Sera didn't look up from her plate.

"Something about you and Jordan Serenghetti being

an item," her mother went on. "I told my hairdresser that the press must have snapped you together because of some invite from your cousin Marisa. You're related by marriage these days, after all."

Yup, and bound to stay that way. It was a gloomy prospect. She was destined to see Jordan again and again. Some traitorous part of her longed to see him again—still—but at the same time, she knew it would be unbearable to maintain a brave front.

"So am I right?" her mother asked brightly, glancing from her to a studiously silent Dante, who'd arrived for the family meal only minutes before.

"It wasn't an event that Marisa was hosting," Sera mumbled.

"And then Natalie—that's my hairdresser—also said she'd heard that Jordan had fathered a child with some woman recently." Rosana Perini heaved a sigh. "Honestly, Natalie hears the worst gossip."

Sera's face grew hot. "Yes, I heard the same story."

Her mother paused and blinked. "You did?"

Sera played with her food. "The photographer who trailed me and Jordan to the movie theater mentioned it."

"Where the Serenghettis were having an outing and invited you. How nice."

Sera held her mother's gaze. "Where Jordan and I were going, just the two of us." *After spectacular sex.*

Dante coughed.

Rosana tilted her head, puzzlement drawing her brows together. "So the story is true? You and Jordan have been dating?"

"Yes."

"And now it turns out he's fathered a child with an-other woman?"

Sera felt her face heat again. Put that way, it sounded like just another scrape that, in her family's eyes, *poor Sera* would get herself into. "That's what the press is saying."

Her mother seemed to be floundering, unsure of how to process what she was hearing. "You didn't tell me that you and Jordan…were seeing each other."

Right. Precisely to avoid situations like this.

"But he's been injured…" Her mother's voice trailed off, as if shock had left her at a loss for words.

"I've been giving him physical therapy." *And more.*

An uncomfortable silence hung in the air so that every tinkle of a fork sounded loud and clear.

Dante cleared his throat. "Sera got mixed up with Jordan because she was helping me out."

Rosana's bewildered expression swung to her son.

"I asked Sera to take on Jordan as a client so I could look better at work." Dante shrugged. "You know, new job and all."

Sera threw her brother a grateful look. For a long time, she'd been out to stake her independence and competence, and these days her family—or at least one of them—seemed ready to acknowledge her help.

"I don't know what to say," her mother said after a pause.

"Don't worry, Mom," Sera said quickly, because old habits died hard and she still felt the need to re-assure her mother. "Jordan and I are no longer seeing each other."

"Because of the story that's circulating?" Rosana asked.

"That was part of it. More because it took me by surprise. *He didn't feel the need to tell me.*"

Her mother sighed.

Dante helped himself to some more meatballs from the serving bowl. "Well, the world has tilted on its axis," he joked. "Sera is bailing me out these days, and Mom has a beau."

"What?" It was Sera's turn to look surprised.

Her mother suddenly looked flustered.

Dante cracked a smile. "Mom's not the only one who has her sources among the town gossips. The gentleman caller is alleged to be a mild-mannered accountant by day, and one mean parlor cardplayer by night."

Sera tilted her head. "Let me guess. You ran into one of Mom's friends from her monthly card-playing posse?"

"Yeah," Dante said slyly. "One of them let it slip. In her defense—" her brother paused to throw their mother a significant look "—Mom's friend thought I already knew."

"Wow," Sera said slowly, her gaze roaming from her brother to her mother and back. "Anyone else have any secrets to share?"

Dante swallowed his food. "Not me. I play it straight."

Sera resisted rolling her eyes. And then, because her mother continued to look embarrassed, she added, "I'm happy for you, Mom. Really happy. It's about time."

"Thank you, Sera," her mother said composedly before raising her eyebrows at Dante. "We're taking things slowly, despite any rumors your brother may be spreading."

Dante just grinned cheekily.

Her mother then focused on Sera again, fixing her with a concerned look. "Are you okay? This must be a lot to deal with."

"I'm a grown-up, Mom. I can manage."

Rosana Perini suddenly smiled. "I know you are, but if you want to talk, I'm here." She waved a hand. "I realize Marisa has been your confidante, but ever since your father died, I think I know something about being the walking wounded."

Sera tried a smile, but to her surprise it wobbled a little. She couldn't help being touched. First Dante, now her mother. It seemed her family was finally able to give her space as an adult—as well as owning up to their own weaknesses. Her mother showed signs of moving on from her fears after the death of a child and, more recently, of a husband. "Thanks, Mom."

Her mother reached across to give her hand a reassuring squeeze and then stood to take some empty plates to the kitchen.

When their mother had departed, Dante threw Sera a curious look from across the table. "So, you and Jordan..."

"Yes?"

Dante leaned forward, keeping his voice low. "Let me know if I need to challenge Serenghetti to a duel. Job or no job, family comes first."

"Thanks, but I've got this."

"I thought...the bet."

"I know. We patched things up. He seemed to have

real feelings for me." *Feelings* again. She was starting to sound like Bernice and Marisa.

"So things were getting real between you and Jordan, and then this happened." Dante cursed.

She leaned forward, too. "He said he doesn't know if he's the father."

Her brother sighed. "For what it's worth, celebrity sports stars are targets for gold diggers and fame seekers all the time. Don't believe everything you read. It might not be true."

Jordan had said as much—or tried to—but at the time, his argument had paled in significance to the parallels to Neil. Except the similarity to Neil wasn't exactly right. Because…because—

"So Jordan has feelings for you. How do you feel about him?"

I love him.

Sera's heart thudded in her chest. She finally admitted to herself what had lingered on the edges of her consciousness despite her pain. Jordan made her sad, mad and bad but vibrantly alive. Sexual tension had given way under her feet like thin ice once she'd gotten to know him.

Yes, she'd been hurt and angry about hearing the bombshell news from a stranger instead of Jordan himself. But unlike her former boyfriend, Jordan hadn't tried to cover up the fact of a secret family for months. And didn't she want to be part of his life, child or no child?

Seeming to read the emotions flitting across her face, Dante continued, "Ser, if you do care about him, you have to figure out what to do."

Sera stared at her brother, and then as their mother reentered the dining room, both she and Dante sat back.

She loved Jordan. The question was: What was she going to do about it?

Fourteen

"I've got news," Marv announced.

"No news is good news," Jordan joked, holding the phone to his ear, "but I'm prepared for anything you have to say. So what did you find, Marv?"

Despite his easygoing tone, Jordan tensed. He'd taken a break from his physical-therapy exercises in his home gym as soon as he'd noticed who was calling. Now the stillness in his apartment on this weekday morning enveloped him. His heart pounded hard against the walls of his chest. Marv's answer had the potential to change his life. If he were already a father, any future—with or without Sera—would be more complicated and a big departure from his life up to now.

He'd agreed to take a paternity test but had told

Marv to hire a private investigator and get back to him once they had a fuller story. He could tell a moment of reckoning was upon him.

"I can say with certainty you're not the father. It's not just the paternity test, but other information that's come to light."

Jordan took a deep breath and lowered his shoulders, the tension whooshing out of him like air from a punctured balloon. Then he silently cursed.

His life had been a roller coaster recently. On top of everything else, Lauren Zummen had given a salacious interview to *Gossipmonger* about their meeting and her subsequent pregnancy.

Jordan winced just thinking about Sera reading that piece. Not that he'd seen her. Bernice had reassigned him to another physical therapist, and he didn't have to ask why.

"Jordan?"

"Yeah, I'm here."

"Lauren wasn't pregnant."

Jordan paced around the gym, wandering aimlessly. "What? How can that be?"

"Her identical twin is the mother of the baby. It took some digging, but the private investigator checked records and talked to people in the small town near Albany that Lauren grew up in."

"What?" He was outraged. "How did they think they were going to get away with this?"

"They weren't. But maybe they'd get a lucrative payment or two from the gossip press for their story and some fame."

"I'm surprised they didn't go for the old-fashioned

blackmail route," Jordan remarked drily, curbing another surge of anger. "You know, make me pay hush money."

"Too risky. They're smart enough to know you could have called their bluff and gotten law enforcement involved. The end result would have been a jail sentence."

Jordan tightened his hold on the receiver. "We've got to get the facts out there. At least the fact that I'm not the father."

"I know, I know."

"Wait until *Gossipmonger* finds out they may have paid for a false story."

"The women are identical twins. They can easily come up with some explanation for why they told the story that they did. Given the timing, you couldn't be ruled out as the father. And the women could claim that they swapped identities three years ago for some reason. That the one you met called herself Lauren but was actually her identical twin, and you didn't know it. The possibilities are endless." His agent paused. "Anything to keep the payments they might have received."

"You've got some insight into the criminal mind," Jordan joked.

"Well, I've been talking to the private investigator, and I've been in the business of representing famous people for a long time."

Jordan took a moment to compose himself. "Thanks, Marv. For everything."

The older man gave a dry chuckle. "It's what I do. A sports agent's work is never done. But for the record, you've been a lot easier to work with than some of my other clients. No secret plastic surgery, no sex tape, no drugs."

"Great for the endorsement deals and the contract that are coming up for negotiation."

"Yup."

"I'm a veritable angel."

Marv chuckled. "Go enjoy the rest of your life, Jordan. If your physical therapist keeps working wonders, we'll be in a good bargaining position."

After he hung up with his agent, Jordan reflected on Marv's last words.

Go enjoy the rest of your life. Marv's news today should have lifted the heavy cloud he'd been under, but somehow he still felt dejected and incomplete.

Jordan raked his hand through his hair and cast a glance around the room. He hadn't bothered mentioning to Marv that Sera was no longer his physical therapist.

She'd worked wonders on him all right, though, and not just with his knee.

He was changed. *She'd* changed him.

Because he loved her.

With a cooler head, and without the issue of possible paternity clouding his judgment, he acknowledged that, given her past experience with men, Sera might easily have felt betrayed by his not initially sharing certain allegations with her. Instead, she'd found out the story from a paparazzo.

He was not that much better than Neil, whoever he was. And wherever the other guy was, Jordan wanted to plant his fist in his face.

Jordan figured his own playboy past hadn't helped

him in gaining Sera's trust. He hadn't even remembered their spring-break encounter at the beach, though she definitely had. But he wasn't the same guy he'd been in his twenties or at the beginning of his relationship with Sera—or even a few weeks ago when he'd been brushing off Marc Bellitti's teasing at the Puck & Shoot.

He'd closed himself off from deep involvement—wanting to have fun at the height of his fame and fortune. But Sera was different. She'd challenged him and made him think about the man he was behind the facade of the well-known professional athlete—until his only choice had been to kiss her and fall all the way in love with her.

Crap. His long-standing rule of keeping to casual relationships hadn't protected him—from a gold digger, a paternity claim or anything else. And now, with Sera, he hadn't just *broken* his rule, he'd exploded it with dynamite. By falling in love with a woman who currently wanted nothing to do with him.

He had to do something about that.

The Puck & Shoot was familiar territory, so it was ridiculous to be tense. She knew that booth two had a rip in its seat cushion and that table four had a chip on its corner. She'd been here a million times.

Except she'd agreed to help out Angus again—and Jordan Serenghetti had just parked himself at table four. Alone.

He looked healthier and stronger than ever. Firm jaw, perfect profile, dark hair that she'd run her fingers through while moaning with desire…

Damn it.

She'd underestimated the power of his appeal. The time that they'd spent apart had either dulled her memory or whetted her appetite.

Still, she tried to draw strength from the crowded environment. At least they weren't completely by themselves.

Sure, she'd been doing some thinking since that night at the movie theater, but seeing him here now was sudden and she wasn't prepared. She expected him to be keeping a low profile with the gossip in the press, and Angus had assured her that he hadn't seen Jordan in a while.

Jordan turned, and his gaze locked with hers.

Steeling herself, notepad at the ready, she approached. "Are you ready to order?"

Her voice sounded rusty to her own ears. This was beyond awkward. Only the fact that she had a job to do kept her moving forward. When they'd parted, accusations had flown and feelings had been hurt. She'd nursed a bruised heart.

"Sera."

Not Angel. Why was he sitting alone when a few of his teammates were at the bar? "What do you want?"

The words fell between them, full of meaning. Then recovering, she nodded at the menu.

"I want to explain."

Flustered, she looked around them. "This isn't the time or place."

"It's beyond time, and it's the perfect place." One side of his mouth lifted in a smile. "And unless you conk me on the head with a menu, I'm in great shape."

She perused him. Unfortunately for her, he was as attractive as ever. Square jaw, laughing eyes, hot body. And Bernice had mentioned that he was continuing to recover well—though Sera had made a point of not asking.

"Fortunately for you," she sniffed, "I'd hate for my hard work in whipping you into shape to be undone."

Jordan laughed, and Sera crossed her arms.

"You have made me better," he said softly. "In more ways than one."

Sera swallowed and dropped her arms. *Ugh.* He could make her mad one minute and want to cry the next.

She glanced around, making sure they weren't drawing attention. "I wish you the best of luck sorting things out with…" She didn't know what to say. *Your baby mama? Ex-lover? Former one-night stand?*

Her heart squeezed, and she felt short of air. All she could manage were shallow breaths.

"I have."

She blinked. "What?"

He looked at her steadily. "I have sorted things out."

"Oh?"

He nodded. "I should have told you right away about the rumors." He paused. "I'm sorry."

She waved an arm dismissively, suddenly emotional and looking anywhere but at him. "Oh…"

He reached into the pocket of his jeans. "The results of the paternity test came back."

She looked down at the papers in his hand uncomprehendingly, her brain frozen.

"The child isn't mine."

Her gaze flew up to his.

"Lauren isn't even the mother."

Beyond the roaring in her ears, she barely made out Jordan's explanation.

"Thanks to Marv, the press should be posting corrected news stories as we speak." He smiled ruefully. "The gossip sites love a story with unexpected twists and turns."

"How can Lauren not even be the mother?" she asked, dumbfounded.

"Her twin sister is."

"How did they think they'd get away with this?"

Jordan's expression darkened. "That was my question. They had to know they'd eventually be found out, but maybe not before they received a fat payment or two to print a juicy story."

Feeling a tremor, she dropped her notepad on the table. "For the record, it doesn't matter. I already made up my mind that whether you were a father already or not was beside the point."

"Sera, I love you."

What? She'd pitched a revelation at him, and he'd hit it right back. And then, because it was all too much and she couldn't think of what else to say, she blurted, "Why should I believe you?"

Jordan stood up and moved closer. "Because you love me, too."

He said it so casually, she almost didn't process the words.

She blinked against a well of emotion and lifted her chin. "Does it matter? You're still…who you are, and I'm who I am."

"And who am I?" he queried, his voice low. "I'm a changed man—"

She opened her mouth.

"—especially since my casual remarks here to Marc Bellitti." He looked contrite.

They both knew which remarks he was referring to.

"At the time, it still seemed safer to play the game, or try to, rather than acknowledge the truth."

"Which is?"

"I love you." He glanced around them and then signaled the bartender.

Sera's eyes grew round. Now they were really creating a scene. "What are you doing? I have to take the order at my next table."

A slight smile curved Jordan's lips. "Already taken care of." He signaled again to someone across the room. "Angus has you covered with another waiter."

"He's short-staffed!"

"Not anymore he isn't. Another employee just stepped out of the back room."

Sera snapped her mouth shut. "You planned—"

"Let's just say Angus is a romantic at heart who's happy to lend a helping hand."

"He called me in when he didn't need me."

"I need you," Jordan said, looking into her eyes. "I've had a chance to sort out my priorities lately. And I've figured out what's important to me besides the career and whether I recover from my injury."

After he gave a sign to the bartender, the music was turned off, and everyone stopped talking. In the sudden stillness, Jordan raised his voice. "I'd like everyone's attention."

Bewildered and worried for him—was it fever? A momentary bout of insanity?—Sera leaned close and whispered, "What are you doing?"

He gave his trademark devilish smile. "In lieu of a jumbotron or big screen…"

OMG.

"I'm making a public declaration—"

Some people hooted.

"—that I think my teammates never thought they'd hear from me."

There was scattered laughter.

"This should be good," someone called out.

"I'm declaring my undying love for—"

Jordan took her hand and kissed it.

"The Puck & Shoot?" someone else wisecracked.

"Hey, maybe it's Angus or his beer." One patron elbowed another.

"Nah, Angus has been married for ages," Vince Tedeschi put in.

"—Serafina Perini," Jordan finished.

"Aww."

"Makes my heart flutter." Marc Bellitti clutched his chest dramatically.

Several women gave audible sighs.

Jordan turned to the peanut gallery lining the far side of the bar, including Vince and Marc. "Hey, guys, knock it off. This is difficult enough. Wearing my heart on my sleeve with no clue about my chances…"

Sera swallowed hard because she'd been getting choked up. Jordan was putting it all on the line for her—in public. She could spurn him, make him pay… or confess that she loved him, too.

Jordan opened his mouth to say more, and Sera impulsively leaned forward and shushed him with a kiss. She could feel his surprise, and then he relaxed, his lips going pliant beneath hers as he let her kiss him.

"Aw."

There were a few laughs, and some women gave audible sighs again.

When she broke the kiss, her gaze connected with Jordan's.

"Is that a yes?" he asked.

She nodded and then slid her arms around his neck. "Yes, yes…yes to everything. I'm all in with you." She looked into his eyes. "I love you, Jordan."

"I think I have a new lease on life in professional hockey thanks to you, and with your help, there are going to be new facilities at the hospital, too."

Sera felt her eyes glisten, so to make up for it, she teased, "They're going to name it the Serenghetti Pavilion?"

"Let's talk. Maybe we should name it after our first-born."

"You've got big plans, Serenghetti."

"Yup."

"Our families will go nuts over the news. And our kids would be double cousins with Dahlia."

He pulled her in for another kiss.

There was a smattering of applause around them.

"I love a happy ending," a woman in the crowd commented.

"Hey, who's going to be the most eligible New England Razor now that Serenghetti has retired?"

"Angus is going to start changing the TV channels

from hockey to the feel-good drama of the week," a guy at the bar grumbled.

"What's wrong with that?" a woman beside him demanded.

As they ended their kiss, Sera laughed against Jordan's mouth. *Nothing, nothing at all.*

Epilogue

If someone had told her a year ago that she'd be planning her wedding to Jordan Serenghetti, Sera would never have believed them. Life was good in unexpected ways…

As she stood next to Jordan, Sera surveyed the assorted Serenghettis mingling in Serg and Camilla's Mediterranean-style mansion before the engagement party began. Soon, she'd be one of them. Serafina Perini Serenghetti, or SPS for short. She'd tried out the name numerous times already in her mind, and it always made her heart thrill. It felt right…like she was exactly where she should be.

Of course, the Serenghettis already treated her as one of them. She was Marisa's cousin, but they'd also embraced her as Jordan's fiancée. In fact, they'd been thrilled with news of the engagement months after she and Jordan had reconciled at the Puck & Shoot.

Camilla had exclaimed that she'd known all along that Sera would be a perfect match for her youngest son. Serg had congratulated Jordan on making a wise decision. Cole and Rick had called their brother a lucky man and joked that he'd soon be joining them in the ranks of fatherhood—making Sera flush. And Marisa had been thrilled that she and Sera would be sisters-in-law as well as cousins.

Mia Serenghetti came up and gave Sera's arm a quick squeeze. "Congratulations. I just wanted to say that again before your family and the other guests get here."

"Thanks, Mia."

Glancing at Jordan, Mia added, "You've made my brother very happy…and he'd better behave himself."

"Now that I'm engaged, you're next," Jordan teased.

His sister feigned offense. "How can you say that, after I kept your and Sera's secret at Constance and Oliver's wedding?"

"Simple. Mom. She's ready for her next starring role. Mother of the bride."

Mia rolled her eyes. "Don't jinx me. I'm married to my fledgling design business."

Sera nudged Jordan. "Good luck, Mia. I'll prolong Jordan's wedding planning as long as I can."

Mia threw her a grateful look. "Thanks. I'm glad I'm gaining an additional ally in this family." She gave her brother a baleful look. "It's been rough going."

As Camilla called Mia over with a question, Jordan glanced at his watch. "Your family should be here soon."

Sera squeezed her hands together. Not out of nervousness but excitement. "Yup. And Mom is bringing a date."

Her mother's *male friend*, as Rosana Perini referred to him, had turned out to be a mild-mannered, middle-aged guy with glasses and a quiet sense of humor. Sera had liked him instantly and was glad her mother was taking the next step by inviting him to be her date today.

Dante, of course, wouldn't miss today, either. Once he and their mother had understood that Sera and Jordan had worked out things between them, and how in love they were, they'd been just as excited as the Serenghettis about the relationship. And Dante naturally had been thrilled about becoming the brother-in-law of the Razors' star player.

Sera hooked her arm through Jordan's and beamed at him.

He was having his best season yet with the Razors. And as a result, Marv had had a great negotiating position. In fact, Jordan's new contract with the Razors had exceeded expectations, and his endorsement deals had so far been renewed for impressive sums. The result was that Jordan's plans to fund the rehabilitation facility at Welsdale Children's Hospital were right on track. Even Bernice was happy with all the new sports-team business that Astra Therapeutics was getting after their success with Jordan.

He leaned down to whisper in her ear. "Have I told you recently that I love you?"

"Not in a few hours."

"Maybe it's time to find another cloakroom."

Sera half laughed, half gasped. "We're at our own engagement party."

Jordan straightened and his eyes gleamed. "It wouldn't surprise anyone. And Mia might even be expecting it."

"Something tells me we'll be searching for a cloakroom for the rest of our lives."

Jordan leaned in for a kiss. "I'm counting on it."

* * * * *

*Don't miss a single story
in The Serenghetti Brothers
series!*

Second Chance with the CEO
Hollywood Baby Affair
Power Play

from USA TODAY *bestselling author Anna DePalo!*

Available now from Harlequin Desire!

Get 4 FREE REWARDS!

We'll send you 2 FREE Books <u>plus</u> 2 FREE Mystery Gifts.

Harlequin® Desire books feature heroes who have it all: wealth, status, incredible good looks... everything but the right woman.

FREE
Value Over
$20

YES! Please send me 2 FREE Harlequin® Desire novels and my 2 FREE gifts (gifts are worth about $10 retail). After receiving them, if I don't wish to receive any more books, I can return the shipping statement marked "cancel." If I don't cancel, I will receive 6 brand-new novels every month and be billed just $4.55 per book in the U.S. or $5.24 per book in Canada. That's a savings of at least 13% off the cover price! It's quite a bargain! Shipping and handling is just 50¢ per book in the U.S. and $1.25 per book in Canada.* I understand that accepting the 2 free books and gifts places me under no obligation to buy anything. I can always return a shipment and cancel at any time. The free books and gifts are mine to keep no matter what I decide.

225/326 HDN GNND

Name (please print)

Address   Apt. #

City   State/Province   Zip/Postal Code

Mail to the **Reader Service:**
IN U.S.A.: P.O. Box 1341, Buffalo, NY 14240-8531
IN CANADA: P.O. Box 603, Fort Erie, Ontario L2A 5X3

Want to try 2 free books from another series? Call 1-800-873-8635 or visit www.ReaderService.com.

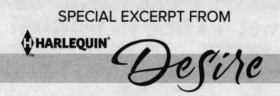
*Developer Tate Duncan has a family he never knew,
and only the sympathy and sexiness of yoga instructor
Hayden Green offers escape. So he entices her into
spending Christmas with him as he meets his birth
parents…posing as his fiancée! But when they give in to
dangerously real attraction, their ruse—and the secrets
they've been keeping—could implode!*

Read on for a sneak peek of
Christmas Seduction
by Jessica Lemmon.

"I don't believe you want to talk about yoga." She lifted
dark, inquisitive eyebrows. "You look like you have
something interesting to talk about."

The pull toward her was real and raw—the realest thing
he'd felt in a while.

"I didn't plan on talking about it…" he admitted, but she
must have heard the ellipsis at the end of that sentence.

She tilted her head, a sage interested in whatever he
said next. Wavy dark brown hair surrounded a cherubic
heart-shaped face, her deep brown eyes at once tender
and inviting. How had he not noticed before? She was
alarmingly beautiful.

"I'm sorry." Her palm landed on his forearm. "I'm
prying. You don't have to say anything."

"There are aspects of my life I was certain of a month
and a half ago," he said, idly stroking her hand with his

thumb. "I was certain that my parents' names were William and Marion Duncan." He offered a sad smile as Hayden's eyebrows dipped in confusion. "I suppose they technically still are my parents, but they're also not. I'm adopted."

Her plush mouth pulled into a soft frown, but she didn't interrupt.

"I recently learned that the agency—" or more accurately, the kidnappers "—lied about my birth parents. Turns out they're alive. And I have a brother." He paused before clarifying, "A twin brother."

Hayden's lashes fluttered. "Wow."

"Fraternal, but he's a good-looking bastard. I just need… I need…" Dropping his head in his hands, he trailed off, muttering to the floor, "Christ, I have no idea what I need."

He felt the couch shift and dip, and then Hayden's hand was on his back, moving in comforting circles.

"I've had my share of family drama, trust me. But nothing like what you're going through. It's okay for you to feel unsure. Lost."

He faced her. This close, he could smell her soft lavender perfume and see the gold flecks in her dark eyes. He hadn't planned on coming here, or on sitting on her couch and spilling his heart out. He and Hayden were friendly, not friends. But her comforting touch on his back, the way her words seemed to soothe the recently broken part of him…

Maybe what Tate needed was her.

What will happen when Tate brings Hayden home for Christmas?

Find out in Christmas Seduction *by Jessica Lemmon. Available October 2019 wherever Harlequin® Desire books and ebooks are sold.*

www.Harlequin.com

Want to give in to temptation with
steamy tales of irresistible desire?

Check out **Harlequin® Presents®,
Harlequin® Desire** and
Harlequin® Kimani™ Romance books!

New books available every month!

CONNECT WITH US AT:

Facebook.com/groups/HarlequinConnection

H HARLEQUIN®

**ROMANCE WHEN
YOU NEED IT**

PGENRE2018

Love Harlequin romance?

DISCOVER.

Be the first to find out about promotions, news and exclusive content!

 Facebook.com/HarlequinBooks

Twitter.com/HarlequinBooks

 Instagram.com/HarlequinBooks

Pinterest.com/HarlequinBooks

ReaderService.com

EXPLORE.

Sign up for the Harlequin e-newsletter and download a free book from any series at **TryHarlequin.com.**

CONNECT.

Join our Harlequin community to share your thoughts and connect with other romance readers!
Facebook.com/groups/HarlequinConnection

**ROMANCE WHEN
YOU NEED IT**

HSOCIAL2018

THE WORLD IS BETTER WITH

Romance

4676

Harlequin has everything from contemporary, passionate and heartwarming to suspenseful and inspirational stories.

Whatever your mood,
we have a romance just for you!

Connect with us to find your next great read, special offers and more.

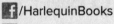

f /HarlequinBooks

🐦 @HarlequinBooks

www.HarlequinBlog.com

www.Harlequin.com/Newsletters